A Killing on Hardee Street

V.S. Gardner

I hope you get caught up in the mystery!
V.S. Gardner

Cover Photo by Vanessa Gardner
Cover Design Created by Germancreative

ISBN 9798695863475

Printed in the United States of America

~ *DEDICATION* ~

*This book is dedicated to **Deb Troiano**.*

With one simple comment Deb reawakened
my childhood dream of becoming a published author.
Once I began to write our emails carried each
written chapter to Deb and her input back to me.
We shared the fun of brainstorming, editing, meeting the characters
and following the unfolding story together.
Her enthusiastic response every step of the way
encouraged me to continue writing.
I am forever grateful for the hours and effort
Deb spent on this project.
The successful publication of this, my first book,
is shared with her.

Deb,
I treasure your across-the-miles friendship;
faithful prayer partnership and unending support.
I am so thankful for the laughter, tears and love
we've shared and will in the years to come.
God knew what He was doing when He brought us together.

Thank you for being my 'something else' on this project.
I love you, dear friend!

~ ACKNOWLEDGEMENTS ~

~ To the one who listened to my ideas and brainstormed with me from beginning to end in this writing, the man whose love has proven pure and lasting, my best friend/husband; **Steven.** Your constant love, entertaining sense of humor, and faithful support mean everything to me! Thank you for always being there to share the trials & joys of life. I love you beyond words and you, more than anyone, know how extensive mine are.

~ To our children whose support and encouragement are such a blessing: **Nathan, Megan & Sam, Jeremy & Janet, Amber & Dan.** Thank you for believing in my dreams. I am thankful for & love each one of you.

~ To those who witnessed my childhood dream and encouraged me through this project: My parents and sisters, **George, Dorma, Debbie & Monica.** Your love and support have carried me through the ups and downs of life & I'm so thankful we're family. I love you.

~ To all extended family & friends who've encouraged me from the sidelines. Thank you & I hope you enjoy this finished product.

~ To those who've offered professional input and guidance.
Editors: **Audrey Polzer, Amanda Williams**
Reader: **T Moise**
Authors: **Linda Amick Algire, Chris Hepner**
Grief Share Leader: **Helen Rossman**
Something Else**: Deb Troiano**

~ *Above all I give thanks to God, my loving Father, for the fulfillment of this dream, the many blessings He continuously pours into my life and for giving me the gift of faith and a way with words.*

My appreciation knows no bounds!

A Killing on Hardee Street

V.S. Gardner

vi

CHAPTER 1

The eyes looking up at him were cold and dead. Was that possible? No, it wasn't. And yet, somehow, *it was true.*

What happened? Frantically his mind searched for the answer. He remembered his rage, seeing Victor go down, shouting at him to get up, to face him; this wasn't over, not by a long shot! His anger growing fiercer he'd covered the short distance between them still shouting for Victor to get up. Then for the first time his own eyes had met the cold, dead, vacant eyes he was looking into right now.

It was taking a few seconds but his mind was beginning to register that Victor was indeed dead. Even now he couldn't believe what was happening. He couldn't accept it as even the remotest of possibilities. And yet each passing second forced him to face reality. Finally, he listened for breath. Finding none he felt for a pulse. Nothing.

His mind exploded "What have you done?" he asked himself. "What have you done? Oh, dear God, what have you done?"

They'd been arguing. That was all. People argue all the time. *No one was supposed to die.* But here he was now standing over Victor's lifeless body.

He raked his hand through his thick dark hair and paced back and forth totally unaware of the sweat streaming down his back. When he stopped to stare at the body the muscles in his legs began to twitch. A nervous reaction he supposed, momentarily distracted.

What was he going to do? Oh, what was he going to do now?

For the briefest of moments he considered calling the police. But no, that was out of the question. He'd worked too hard to get to this point in his life. Everything was going great for him. He couldn't lose it all now. He *wouldn't!*

No. There was absolutely no question about it. No one could know what had happened here tonight. No one could *ever know.*

He began to pace again trying to calm himself.

"Pull yourself together, man," he said aloud as he began to take stock of the situation.

If no one was to know, he was going to have to deal with the body. Yes, that was it. He just had to pull himself together and deal with the situation at hand. Just the way he'd done all his life. This was no different.

As his mind started to clear he studied Victor's still figure again, mentally noting that there was no blood. That would make things simpler.

He'd been working late. Being as it was well after regular hours everyone had gone home. He had, in fact, been startled when Victor first spoke. Victor had entered quietly coming up behind him so quietly he hadn't even realized anyone was there. When was that? Glancing at his watch; just twenty minutes ago. He hadn't heard Victor arrive. Was there a car to deal with? There must be. Where were the keys? What was he going to do about the car?

What else might place Victor here with him tonight? He would have to find out and deal with it. He'd have to deal with *all of it*. If he was going to cover this up, *and he was*, he'd have to be thorough. *Nothing* could be overlooked. *No trace of Victor could be left behind.*

Without even fully realizing what he was doing, he began to formulate a plan. Glancing at his watch again, his mind began to itemize each step of what he was about to do.

At some now distant, future time, when he looked back on these moments it would be with amazement at how easily and quickly the decision had been made and how methodically he'd done what he'd decided he must.

He may not realize it right now but this was a defining moment in his life.

A moment; like all moments, that once lived, could never be changed.

CHAPTER 2
SIX MONTHS EARLIER

Vonda yawned and stretched her arms over her head as she began to come to life. As was true every morning her mind immediately went to prayer.

"Thank you for another day, God," she said aloud as she stretched her legs, throwing aside the covers and sitting up on the edge of the bed. "Thank you that I rested well. I even slept straight through."

That hadn't often been the case in recent months.

"Good morning, Lilly" she said as her beautiful white, long hair cat, whom she'd named after her favorite flower; the white Easter Lily, gently pounced onto the bed and nuzzled up beside her. Lilly's head rose and dipped with each stroke of her owner's hand.

Vonda stood, stretched, walked two feet forward and opened the blinds of her bedroom window. Daylight flooded in. Without a doubt her favorite feature of this house was the large picture windows in the master bedroom and main living area.

A few moments later hot water in the shower beat down upon her. Vonda silently named each of her grown children as she talked them over with God. Asking him to watch over them, to continue to bless them with good health and safety, to help them learn from life's difficulties and bask in its joys.

Stepping from the shower she wrapped her shoulder length hair into a towel and piled it on top of her head. She then dried off and stepped into her clothing. She walked to the kitchen and set a K-cup to brewing. Unwrapping her hair she couldn't help noticing there were now more white strands running through the light brown. She quickly combed it into place as the strong smell of her morning coffee beckoned.

She filled Lilly's food dish and stroked the length of her a few more times. Vonda poured a cup of coffee and put the hot mug to her lips, savoring the flavor as she lazily walked over to the sliders facing the back yard. Leaning gently into the door her eyes scanned the empty lots next to her property. They sought out the new construction taking place approximately five lots away over on Hardee Street. Hardee Street ran perpendicular to Anderson Avenue which Vonda's house sat on. There were empty lots to one side and

3

behind her house. This gave Vonda a clear view of Hardee Street from her back patio.

Pulling a shrug across her shoulders to ward off the morning chill she slid the door open. Sinking into the rocking chair on the back patio she began to sip her coffee. This had quickly become her morning habit. Vonda enjoyed keeping up with the progress on the new house being built in her neighborhood. She relaxed into place watching the men frame up the walls of what would be someone's home in the not too distant future.

As she thought of the family that would one day live there she prayed simply; "Bless them, Lord."

A smiled played at her lips as she remembered the new home she and Stanley had built together so many years ago. What an exciting time that had been in their lives. Every day one of them would drive by their new home and report to the other what progress was being made.

She'd never forget the day the roof went on. Unbeknownst to her Stanley had driven by on his way to work that morning. He'd seen the workers laying the first sheets of plywood. A few short hours later while running errands Vonda had succumbed to the urge to drive by the house herself. Overcome with excitement at the two workers walking on the new roof she'd immediately called her husband.

"Stanley..." no one called him that but her. To all the rest of the world he was just Stan. But to Vonda he was Stanley.

"Stanley, you won't believe this...." she'd started.

To her surprise he said it with her "...they're laying the roof today!"

They'd laughed in unison.

Precious memories. Even now all these years later, in her mind's eye Vonda could still see those two men walking on that roof, the sun shining in the distance. The snow was covering the disrupted earth in the foreground and all around the new house.

That morning, she'd sat there in her car, by the side of the road, asking God to bless them in that house. Asking him to heal the hurts they had so recently endured. To use them to bind herself and Stanley together with a strength that nothing they may face in the future could tear apart.

"Thank you for answering those prayers, Father," she now said aloud.

"You certainly did bless us in that house. You gave us so many happy years there. And the way you moved us on to the next stage of life was nothing short of miraculous."

They'd built the house planning to live there for the rest of their lives.

Of course, the children grew up and one by one moved on to pursue their own dreams. The way it's been since the beginning of time. The way it's meant to be.

Vonda's memories rushed onward to the day everything had changed.

CHAPTER 3

She and Stanley were well on their way to Pennsylvania. They were going to see the newly erected memorial at the spot where the plane went down on nine eleven in two thousand one. It was a beautiful sunny day and they chatted about everything and nothing. Stanley expertly guided the car along.

She couldn't remember, after the fact, which of them had first broached the subject of moving. She must have since Stanley had sounded so surprised. He said he thought she loved their house and would never consider moving.

She thought that through a few seconds before answering "I do love the house. But I love you more and I can live anywhere and be happy as long as we're together. Besides, the children are gone now and it's more house than we need for just the two of us. Not to mention ten acres takes a lot of upkeep and we're both getting older. I know we don't like to think about that, but we are!"

He laughed at that even as he admitted it was getting harder to keep everything done and he was feeling it.

Before they knew it they were chatting about new possibilities.

Vonda remembered the feelings of excitement and adventure that had built up inside her. That is, until Stanley said; "But without a well our house will never sell."

They bought the property after extensive research showed all the surrounding properties had a personal well. A strong indication there was an underground water source for their property. Unfortunately, after three attempts, each one pricey, no water had been found. Out of options, they went with an underground cistern. When the house was built the spouting system fed into the cistern. It passed through a filtering system so the water was useable, even drinkable. Unfortunately, a few years later a huge storm caused the water to backflow into the cistern. It wasn't safe for drinking after that.

Stanley had made a good point. Who would buy a house without its own water source? Ever calling upon her faith Vonda had simply answered, "Let's pray about it and see how God leads us."

And that is exactly what they did. By the time they returned home they were in agreement. They would list the house and trust God for whatever was to be. After that God's plan for their future had simply unfolded.

The first couple to view their house absolutely fell in love with it. The miraculous part was that they'd been renting a place for seven years that didn't have drinkable water. They were used to buying bottled water and had no problem continuing to do so.

The couple paid the asking price. Just three short months from the day they listed the old house Vonda and Stanley were settling into their new home. Stanley laughingly said, "God was surely amused at how long it took us to realize it was time to move on. The way it all fell into place once we listed the house made it obvious He'd had that planned all along."

Vonda was thankful she could still hear Stanley's laughter in her memories. When he'd passed away so suddenly she'd been afraid it would be forgotten.

The sun had begun to warm the day so Vonda laid her shrug inside. She then locked the door and headed out to run her errands.

CHAPTER 4

Vonda listened to a bit of talk radio as she prepared a chicken breast marinated in an Italian dressing. It would serve as a late lunch/early supper. She was thinking about taking a walk after eating. She and Stanley had been active while raising their family. Once the children were grown they'd taken to walking in an effort to remain healthy as they continued to age.

They hiked often at the local state park and made it a point to visit state parks when vacationing. Even though she'd lost him and didn't go hiking anymore Vonda knew Stanley would want her to remain active and healthy.

In the days following his death she'd been overcome with grief and the walking had stopped, along with just about everything else. Vonda had eventually learned that contrary to the popular saying; time *doesn't* heal all wounds. But *it does help*. It took some time but eventually she'd started walking again. It definitely wasn't the same but it was important. So she walked. Not every day, but many.

She put her walking shoes on and set out on her way. Vonda remembered what fun they'd had searching for just the right house to be their last home before heaven. They laughed together when they said that because it *wasn't the first time* they'd said it. If there was one thing they had learned together along the way it was that life has a way of proving us wrong.

They had always planned to retire in a warm climate, somewhere close to the ocean where the sun would beat down on them and they could enjoy walking on the beach. When their children were small they'd often joked that one day they would end up living closest to whichever of the children lived in a warm climate.

They were blessed to make that move when Stanley's job transferred him. They were happy to leave the heavy traffic behind since the move wasn't only to a warmer climate but to a smaller town; the small community of Logan, SC, which Vonda now called home.

Terming the move an adventure Stanley and Vonda had enjoyed every part of it. Even now Vonda found joy in reminiscing. Although, she'd been alone for just over a year it was still a struggle. She was doing much better and believed she was finally beginning to find her new normal.

Over the past year she'd seen that doing things she and Stanley had done together was helpful for her, things as simple as taking walks. Besides, it was good for her physically and was a simple way for her to get out into the community. Just to see people and integrate more into this place that was now her home.

Vonda couldn't deny being lonely. After all, they hadn't lived in Logan very long when she lost Stanley. Even though she'd met many people through her church she was still a bit isolated and that just wasn't good. Those were her thoughts as she walked along until the sounds of people shouting suddenly broke in.

"Go, Go! *Go!!"* they shouted in unison, excitement filling their escalating voices.

She'd taken to walking through her neighborhood crossing over one street to where she'd pass by a children's park, baseball field and the public pool. She'd then circle back toward home.

She was near the baseball field now and a little league game was winding down to an apparent big finish. She rushed over to the fence line just in time to see the little fellow round third base.

"Go *home!*" the crowd shouted in unison as the outfielder finally landed the ball. Vonda found herself getting caught up in the excitement as she watched the little guy throw his legs out in front of him and slide into home plate just seconds before the ball hit the catcher's mitt.

"SAFE!!" the umpire shouted throwing his arms straight out in the universal signal as the crowd went wild.

The years fell away as Vonda remembered her own excitement as the mother whose own son had just slid into home plate. Her eyes sought out the glowing face of this boy's mom in the crowd. She was shouting, "That's my boy. That's *my* boy! Good job, Nathan! *Greeeaaat play, son!!"*

Vonda stayed by the fence and took it all in as the game wound down and ended. Being near the dugout she enjoyed watching the parents collect their players. Many treated them to something special at the concession stand before heading to their vehicles.

A short while later Vonda entered her front door and quickly entered the code to her alarm system. She realized she wasn't feeling quite so lonely. For the first time in a long time, she wasn't thinking about how empty the house felt. She was instead, replaying that home run in her mind.

She was glad she'd taken a walk this evening. It had done her good. Feeling the sunshine, stretching her legs and seeing everyone enjoying themselves at the ball field had lifted her spirits.

"Thank you, Lord, for this very good day," she said softly as she settled into her recliner. Lilly gently jumped into her lap and settled in beside her as Vonda picked up her book and found her place. She read a few chapters before nodding off in her chair.

An hour or so later she slipped off to bed.

CHAPTER 5

"OK men, grab a donut and let's get this meeting started," Marshall's deep voice boomed as he unceremoniously dropped the box of Krispie Kremes in the middle of the conference room table. His construction crew wasn't accustomed to meeting at the downtown office so he tried to keep things casual when it was required.

"The Hardee Street Project is coming along well," he continued, as the men got settled around the table.

He could always count on DeeDee to make the guys comfortable with her easy, cheerful, banter while they waited for Marshall to arrive. He could tell by their relaxed demeanor that today had been no exception.

Marshall wasn't sure which trait was more important in his Office Manager. Having the personality to handle the variety of people the construction industry brought together or having excellent administrative skills. All he knew was that he'd gotten darn lucky the day she applied to join his team. Having worked together almost twenty years now they had an easy rapport. Despite her flaming red hair DeeDee had a remarkably calm temperament and worked well under pressure. She always dressed and handled herself professionally, yet she had an uncanny ability to put everyone at ease. Each trait made her a real asset to the company.

After updating them on various changes in the current projects, Marshall turned the meeting over to the company accountant, Victor. He was now going over a few items in regard to supply requisitions and purchasing invoices. Victor had been an excellent addition to the staff when Marshall's original accountant retired over a year ago. In his mid-twenties Victor was inexperienced in the construction industry but was an excellent numbers guy. He'd quickly applied himself and already seemed to have a good handle on things. As Victor went over a few changes in the ordering process Marshall scanned the faces of his various crew members.

His crew leaders, Manny and Saul, had been with Marshall from the start. The three of them had been thick as thieves as children. They'd actually built a few childhood forts and a pretty impressive tree house together. Each of them worked in the industry after graduating high school. When Marshall decided to start his own construction firm it had only seemed natural to talk with his two friends about joining the team. Having the two of them to lead

11

the crews sure simplified the process of having multiple projects, which was happening more frequently as the company grew. The three men had met prior to this morning's meeting. They always took the opportunity to compare notes whenever the three crews met at Corporate.

Next there was Carlos, Manny's nephew. Carlos was one of the newest and youngest crew members to come on board. They'd offered him a position when the work load had picked up and he seemed to be working out well. Then, there was Mitch; Marshall's brother. Mitch had worked for several other construction crews before joining Marshall's firm. He'd been with the company for over ten years now. Mitch didn't know it yet, but he was in line to be the next crew leader if the company continued to expand.

As he continued along the table, Marshall realized for the first time that Mason was seated next to Mitch. He felt a sudden sense of pride at having both of his younger brothers on his crew for the first time since starting the company over twenty five years earlier.

To his surprise, and for a brief moment, Marshall struggled against an unusual tug of emotion as he thought of how proud their Dad would be.

He was certain it hadn't been noticed but he turned away to peer out the window just long enough to regain his emotional composure.

Their father had taught Marshall everything he knew. Marshall attributed his business success completely to the man, his success as an older brother and mentor, too, for that matter. Their mother had suffered a miscarriage after having Marshall and it was quite a few years before she'd conceived again. At eight years old Marshall was a big help when the new baby, Mitch, came along. Of course, their mother had fostered feelings of protectiveness in the older boy and often bragged at what an excellent big brother he was.

Several years later when Mason was born Marshall again was very helpful. There was no denying he'd fallen into the big brother role quite well early in life. He truly loved his little brothers. Despite the wide gap in their ages he had fond memories of playing with them during childhood. That is, when he wasn't off building things with Manny and Saul. Actually, the older boys had often let the younger boys tag along. His friends had been quite accepting of his brothers as he had of theirs. It was another story when it came to Saul's sisters. The boys had no interest in them, at least not until years later.

Marshall was only twenty five when a tragic car accident claimed the lives of his parents and it fell to him to finish raising his younger brothers. Mitch had just turned seventeen and Mason was fourteen. It was a huge responsibility but Marshall didn't even hesitate. He knew his parents would have expected it and he wasn't about to let his brothers be separated or put into foster care.

It hadn't been easy, especially with no extended family support, but they'd muddled through. Marshall wasn't ashamed to admit he had actually breathed a huge sigh of relief at Mason's High School graduation. It was a relief when the active role he'd played in his brother's upbringing was no longer a necessity.

After graduating Mason continued to struggle trying to find his way in life. It was a struggle that lasted through the years, especially professionally. After his most recent career shakeup and separating from his wife Mason asked Marshall if he could join his two older brothers at Davidson Construction. Marshall had extended the offer to both of his brothers on several occasions through the years. This was the first time Mason had shown even the slightest interest. Marshall was happy to have Mason on board, even though he'd been a bit uncertain as to how it was going to work out. But Manny and Saul, and even Mitch, had approved the motion and were now assuring him Mason was adapting well.

As far as Marshall could see Mason certainly seemed to be seriously applying himself to learning the ins and outs of the construction trade. The crew leaders would attest that he was doing an honest day's work each day. To Marshall's great relief Mason was earning his pay and seemed to be finding his place on the crew.

Yes, their father would be *very proud*. Marshal thought again as Victor finished his presentation and turned the meeting back over to him. After a brief question and answer session Marshall dismissed the men to return to their various work sites. Though they'd long since become grown men Marshall couldn't resist slapping his little brothers on their backs good naturedly, one after the other, as they'd headed out the door. It didn't matter how old they got they'd always be 'the boys' in Marshall's mind.

Half an hour later, Marshall pulled up at the Hardee Street construction project. Seeing Victor's vehicle already there he hurried inside. For Victor's benefit Marshall had arranged for a tour after the meeting. They were all in agreement that since Victor was seldom on site it would serve to show him where the finances were going.

Marshall was a bit surprised when his youngest brother, the newest crew member, Mason, took the lead on the tour. His supervisor, Manny, stayed in the background allowing him to show Victor and Marshall around. Marshall had to admit he was impressed with the way Mason was conducting himself and the knowledge he'd obviously gained since coming on board. It was good to see the accuracy of the reports he'd been getting. Mason pointed out the progress and described the work yet to be completed. He seemed to be proud of his own contribution to this particular project. He was certainly enthusiastic. Had he finally found his niche in the working world, right here with his older brothers? Marshall hoped so. He wanted nothing more than to see his youngest brother find the peace and contentment he and Mitch had gained years earlier.

CHAPTER 6

Vonda had overslept so it was a bit later than usual when she settled into the rocking chair on the back patio. She savored the hot coffee as Lilly sat watching her through the sliders.

Vonda immediately noticed two vehicles she hadn't seen at the construction site before. Through the framed structure she could see four men moving from room to room. The one leading the others was pointing and gesturing, obviously updating the others on the project.

"Lord, please help him remember to cover everything he's supposed to in this meeting," she whispered softly.

Vonda had always enjoyed taking her morning coffee on the back patio. Since the new house had started going up it had become a part of her routine to keep up with the daily progress.

Prayer was such a natural part of her life that she'd soon began praying for the construction crew as she watched them come and go. Sometimes simply asking God to bless them and their families, to keep them safe as they worked on the houses and to draw them to faith in Him or strengthen their existing faith.

The tour had apparently ended and the men went out to inspect the wooden roof trusses that had just been delivered. Seeing those trusses reminded Vonda of Stanley since he'd always built their trusses himself. Of course, they'd only been doing small home additions where these men were building multiple new residences. They may even build commercially for all Vonda knew. It was a business so it only stood to reason.

Vonda smiled as a memory of the first time Stanley built himself a work shed shortly after they'd married came to mind. She had been simply amazed to see the trusses take shape. That was probably when Stanley first realized Vonda didn't have an eye for measurements, angles or distances. She just wasn't able to picture the completed project when looking at the separate parts. Stanley certainly could though. So many times she'd stood in the aisle of the home improvement store watching him hold several items in his hands as he talked himself through how to fit them together. When he was satisfied he had everything needed to complete his current project they made the purchase and headed home.

15

She couldn't help laughing as she remembered the time they'd had to flatten the passenger seat in order to stack all the wooden boards they needed. Vonda stayed in her seat and laid it as flat as she could. Then Stanley slid the boards in from the hatchback trunk. Of course, the boards covered her up. On the drive home they had such fun talking about how virtually invisible she was to others. No one else knew she was even in the car. Oh, how they'd laughed on that trip.

Vonda and Stanley worked so well together that their children jokingly called the home improvement store their parents date destination. Vonda chuckled softly again at that memory.

Through the years she and Stanley had spent a good many hours working side by side. Truthfully though, Vonda mostly just watched as her handsome husband measured and cut each board to size.

"Measure twice, cut once." he often told her as he whipped out his measuring tape and lined up the correct angles. A few moments later, her heartbeat would flutter when he winked at her as he hammered the boards in place. Stanley manually hammered in each nail, even after nail guns became popular. He always took great pride in his work.

The two of them completed so many projects together through the years; closet shelves, sheds, that new garage and breezeway addition onto the old farm house they bought. With each move they'd renovated the kitchen. How many kitchens in all? Was it three or four? It was four, she thought.

Vonda knew she wasn't essential to the projects. All she did was bring more nails, hold a board in place, steady the ladder or fetch whatever tool Stanley needed at the time. But anytime she said she wasn't doing much Stanley assured her he couldn't do the job without her. While she didn't think that was really true, she could admit, at the very least, it would've been more time consuming and difficult without her.

"Besides," he'd always say "I could never find better company than you, Vonda."

Stanley had never failed to make her feel valuable in every area of the life they'd shared. He was such a treasure. What a blessing to have had so many years with him.

It was only after he was gone that Vonda realized how much Stanley had taught her. While holding those boards in place and listening to him reason out his purchases she'd been learning. Stanley would be so proud of her now.

16

Shortly after he'd passed away she needed a new doorknob. She determined then and there she wasn't going to be paying strangers to do simple household repairs she could handle herself. After all the years they'd spent together, no wife of Stanley Graham's should pay a handyman and Vonda wasn't about to if it wasn't absolutely necessary. She put that doorknob in herself and felt really proud when it was done. She could just see Stanley smiling over her, too.

Oh, how she missed the life they had shared, working together, running errands, shell searching on the seashore, quiet evenings at home, just talking, laughing and loving each other through it all. They'd grown together through the years. They had arrived at such a comfortable place after thirty five years of marriage. These were her thoughts as she drank her coffee and looked over at the new home being built on Hardee Street.

Anyone observing her daily routine may take her to be a nosy neighbor but there wasn't a nosy bone in her body. Nosiness wasn't her motivation. This was simply a matter of comfort and reminiscing.

CHAPTER 7

While flipping the calendar page from Friday to Monday it dawned on him that his one year anniversary with Davidson Construction was fast approaching. Since he'd had no prior experience in the construction industry, Victor Tonnae had felt extremely fortunate when Marshall Davidson chose to take a chance on him.

Almost immediately after graduating with his Accounting Degree, Victor had landed an accountant position with one of the largest firms in his home town in the State of Iowa. After five years with the firm, unbeknownst to his superiors and colleagues, Victor found himself in a bit of a rut. Despite being the envy of many of his high school classmates who only saw his College Degree, lucrative income and independent, bachelor lifestyle Victor felt that nothing significant was happening in his life. He found himself pining for something new and adventurous, if not, emotionally fulfilling and lasting. In a moment of discontentment he jumped onto a job search website. The advertisement for a company accountant at Davidson Construction Residential and Commercial Inc. in Stokesbury, South Carolina caught his eye. Doing a quick internet search Victor found and read several articles about the company. He was impressed to see it listed as one of the most promising up and coming businesses in South Carolina.

The position appealed to Victor for several reasons, not the least of which was the CEO Marshall Davidson. Mr. Davidson had a reputation of being a man of integrity. He had apparently stayed true to his humble beginnings while climbing the ladder of success in the business community. Every article included interviews with past and present staff, vendors and even competitors. Each one spoke of their ease in interacting with Mr. Davidson and his genuine appreciation for their contributions and services. Several hinted at the man's philanthropic endeavors, which were always handled with discretion. Obviously, Marshall Davidson wasn't one for looking down on others or seeking personal notoriety, which in Victor's estimation, was quite rare. The position also appealed to Victor due to the apparent sense of security the employees felt within the company. Mr. Davidson valued loyalty from his employees and gave it in return. Victor knew this wasn't true of many companies in the present business world. Victor wanted to work for a business where integrity and fairness were prevalent. He also desired a long-term position where he could build his personal financial security in preparation of having a family of his own. Soon approaching his twenty eighth birthday he had serious hopes of meeting the woman who could become his wife in the not-too-distant future.

The final reason the position was appealing was its location. Victor was ready for an adventure and moving to an area within an hour of a tourist town along the ocean coastline sounded absolutely awesome.

With all of this in mind Victor was unhesitant in submitting his cover letter and resume. All the while telling himself he was symbolically sending it on a wing and a prayer. He realized the chances of it meeting with the approval of Mr. Davidson were slim to none.

Even so, once the resume was submitted Victor found himself feeling excited at the prospects of something new. He kept reminding himself the chance of hearing back for an interview was unlikely. He was an out of state applicant and there had surely been many local applications submitted.

Victor was pleasantly surprised, just two weeks later, to receive an email inviting him to schedule a phone interview. The Company's process was to whittle down the list of applicants by choosing those who would advance to the next step after a successful phone interview.

Correctly so, Victor had felt fairly confidant he'd be hearing from HR after what he considered to have been a successful phone interview.

The next step was a flight to Stokesbury for a face to face interview with Marshall Davidson himself. It was during that interview that Victor learned the company's original accountant was soon retiring. He had, however, agreed to stay long enough to show the incoming accountant the ropes. Victor was very pleased to learn his cover letter had caught Mr. Davidson's eye. It caused him to personally ask that Victor be contacted for the initial phone interview.

When the two men met Victor immediately understood the descriptions of Mr. Davidson he'd read in the researched articles. The man certainly had a way about him. Victor came away from their meeting feeling as if he'd just enjoyed an afternoon with a trusted family friend. Marshall was personable and yet professional at all times.

He may very well be the most genuine man Victor had ever met.

Unlike what Victor's friends had shared with him from the many interviews they'd taken, there were no hypothetical questions asking where he saw himself in five to ten years, what was his most prominent strength and what was his most glaring weakness. Mr. Davidson simply shared his own business background and asked Victor to share his. He genuinely took an interest in Victor's reason for wanting to leave Iowa, move across country and fill a position in which he had no background outside of accounting.

Upon the advice of his friends and colleagues Victor had prepared answers intended to feed the ego of the CEO. Or to pull the wool over his eyes, whichever he deemed necessary to get his foot in the door. They would certainly have declared him a failure if he'd shared that he simply spoke from his heart. Sharing with Mr. Davidson that his life had become dull and he was in search of a new adventure as well as a successful business venture. Even admitting he had no background or knowledge of the construction industry. Further, stating he excelled at learning new things and would apply himself to gain the knowledge he'd need to contribute to the success of Davidson Construction if he were only given the chance.

He'd been surprised when Mr. Davidson asked him to relax a bit while he took another meeting. He promised to get back with him for the remainder of the interview shortly. Victor had felt confident things were going well, which helped him remain relaxed as he'd waited. Still, it was a complete shock when upon his return Mr. Davidson made him an on-the-spot job offer and they hashed out an acceptable agreement. To Victors great pleasure the offer carried an awesome benefits package including three weeks of vacation upon the completion of his first year of service with the company.

The men shook hands and set the dates for Victor to begin his new career with Davidson Construction. According to everyone Victor knew this was simply unheard of in today's industry. On his return flight to Iowa Victor couldn't help but marvel that what had started out on a whim had quickly progressed to an exciting new adventure which was about to unfold.

CHAPTER 8

Watching the progress of the new house on Hardee Street was a constant reminder of the good life Vonda had shared with Stanley. It seemed to her now, as if God had provided them this neighborhood knowing it would help Vonda feel more at home once she was living there alone. Her memories were a constant source of comfort and joy.

Still, Vonda knew she needed more than memories. As time went by she found herself becoming more determined to live the life alone that she and Stanley had planned to live together. She just needed to learn how. She was doing her best to do just that day by day.

Their move to Logan was to have been their final move. Vonda had retired the year before and Stanley only had 5 more years to work. They had planned to get to know the people in the area by attending ball games, joining a church and attending community events. Before they knew it they'd have friends and Logan would feel like home.

They arrived in November. Logan really did it up big for Christmas and it all began with their annual festival in early December. The couple had been excited to attend. It would be fun to watch the children see Santa arrive in town. Vonda loved music and was excited to learn Christmas music was streamed in on the main street throughout the Christmas season, beginning with the festival.

Stanley parked the car near the start of the parade route. They walked the sidewalk the entire length of Main Street until they found a hot chocolate vendor. Stanley bought one for Vonda, who thoroughly enjoyed sipping the steaming beverage while they admired the lighted decorations in the center of town. After locating Santa's house they reversed directions and walked down the center of the street. They held hands and smiled at those who were seated in their lounge chairs along the sidewalks waiting to watch the parade.

Stanley turned to Vonda and said, "No one knows us here."

Vonda laughingly answered, "You're right! Do you suppose in fifteen years we'll do this again and they'll all be saying 'Look there's Stan and Vonda'?"

Stanley smiled. "Nah," he said, "they won't know me - but they'll all know you. You've always had a knack for fitting in."

That memory caused Vonda to wonder, as she sometimes did these days, if Stanley had somehow sensed he wouldn't be with her long, a premonition maybe? Not long after they'd bought the house and gotten settled in Stanley had smiled and commented, "We did good. This house is just the right size for you." She remembered chuckling as she corrected him, "*for us*, Stanley, this house is just the right size *for us* and I totally agree." He had smiled and quietly nodded his agreement.

She hadn't given it much thought at the time but now it sometimes played over in her mind. Whether Stanley had known or not, *God had known* and He had seen her through that terrible time, just as He continued seeing her through each new day, even now.

"Thank you, Father," she said aloud as these thoughts ran through her mind. She *was truly grateful* for all she was blessed with and for getting through those difficult days after losing Stanley.

As the day wore on and Vonda ran her errands and took care of the house she kept thinking of the plans she and Stanley had made when moving here. Their plans had included going to the ball field to watch the games. She'd really enjoyed seeing that young boy slide into home plate last week.

As she put away her supper dishes she decided to walk by the ball park to see if there wasn't a game this very evening. Why not?

Approaching the ball field she could see a few spectators in the stands. Not many though. Upon her arrival she was surprised to see that the ball players weren't children at all. They were grown men, middle-aged actually, some even a bit older. There were quite a few she'd guess to be close to her own age. Interesting, she thought as she climbed a few rows up on the bleachers and took a seat.

The men joked, good-naturedly as they played and she enjoyed listening to them. As the game progressed Vonda was able to connect the few spectators to the man they cheered for. She got caught up in the game. She felt quite comfortable cheering a bit herself as the evening wore on. Whenever she cheered she noticed several of the players looking her way curiously. A few were smiling. *This was quite fun.*

"Alright fellows," one of the men called out as the game ended and they all started off the field. "What d'ya think? Not bad for a first night out, right?" There were a few cheers and a lot of laughter as one of the men interjected "We didn't break any bones and nobody passed out anyway!"

The first man continued "Thanks for signing up for the Old Timers league and coming out tonight. We've got enough for two teams. That's enough for some friendly competition so we're off to a good start. If you're all on board I say we meet here every Thursday. What d'ya say? Are you with me?" There were nods, smiles and agreeable comments all around.

As the men laughed and slapped each other on the shoulders and headed toward their vehicles Vonda made her way off the bleachers and started her walk toward home. Dusk was falling quickly and it was almost completely dark by the time she arrived and locked herself safely inside.

She'd really enjoyed herself and was so glad she'd decided to go. As she went from window to window closing the blinds she was seriously considering going back to watch the fellows play again.

After completing her nightly routine Vonda spent a little time playing with Lilly.

Vonda truly was lonely without Stanley. Fortunately, she'd become quite good at finding something else to focus on. She often reminded herself to just be thankful for the many happy years they'd shared. It wasn't much later that she was lulled her off to sleep by her sweet memories.

CHAPTER 9

Marshall made the turn onto Hardee Street and the first house in that project came into view. He was happy to see it was well under way. The crews should finish it up and start the foundations on the next two lots by the end of next week.

Manny was now heading up two separate crews simultaneously and Mason's coming on board was working out well. The expansion of Davidson Construction had gone even better than anticipated. Sometimes it really is all in the timing Marshall thought as he swung his truck onto the lot.

He jumped out just as Carlos and Mason rounded the corner carrying an extension ladder. It looked like they were getting the insulation wrap started today.

Right on schedule.

Marshall was pleased to hear the easy banter between them as he approached. It's always good when crew members get along.

"Hey, boss man," Mason called out playfully. It did Marshall good seeing his brother cheerful and fitting in comfortably.

Also, it was always good to have the crew comfortable with the boss, which was the main reason Marshall was there. He sprinted past them, grabbed the roll of insulation wrap and caught up to them just as they were getting the ladder set in place.

A few minutes later Saul joined them.

Marshall had learned quickly after starting Davidson Construction that there was much more to the business than the actual hands on parts of the job. As the business took on more projects and began to be profitable Marshall had to wear many hats he hadn't worn before. It's at this point of gaining new knowledge to make the new hats fit that most bosses stop working side by side with their crew. As they take on more corporate responsibilities they let go of the basics. Marshall refused to do that. He loved building and he loved the camaraderie of being part of a construction crew. It was quite the task to stay on top of finances, vendor choices, staff and board meetings and everything else involved in the corporate side of the work while remaining active in the actual process of building. But Marshall was unwilling to stop being part of the crew so he simply never did. Whatever had to be moved around or postponed so he could spend days like today on the projects with the crews was fine with him. He strongly believed working with his men was just as important as everything else. Despite his growing responsibilities through the years he'd always made sure to take a day here and there to join the crew on each project. Working side by side with the men kept him close to the projects and kept the men comfortable with him. This practice was one of the reasons Marshall was well liked by everyone in his company from the top down.

Once the ladder was set it didn't take long for the four men to fall into a smooth operation of getting the wrap stretched out and secured into place. Making short work of it they were well on their way to having the East wall covered when Mitch and Manny showed up with another crew.

Mitch had been with his older brother's company for just over ten years. During that time he'd worked on every construction crew at one time or another and knew every crew member pretty well. Mitch was more in the habit of observing and thinking than talking which wasn't a bad trait to have. His quiet nature went a long way toward helping him get along well with a variety of personalities. It was, of course, well known within the company that he was the owner's brother but that had never affected his working relationships. Mitch had always been a hard worker with a get-the-job-done in the most efficient and practical way attitude. Once the other crew members saw that he was just a regular guy, things always went smoothly.

The crew members who'd known Mitch the longest found it interesting that his younger brother, Mason, was such a talker. Apparently, Mitch was the quiet one, Marshall was somewhere in the middle and Mason was the most talkative of the three brothers.

The afternoon sun might've proven too much but for the wind. It was just strong and consistent enough to beat the heat making for a perfect day in the construction business. Any stronger gusts would've ripped the paper out of their hands before they had a chance to get it secured in place. As it was the wind relieved them from the heat and the house was almost completely covered by the time they stopped to take a late lunch break.

Gathering around the company van, each man pulled their sack lunches out of the lunch cooler. Manny opened the cooler he always kept loaded with water and sodas.

There was a good bit of brow wiping and seat finding. Then Saul regaled them all with an exaggerated tale of Mason's overreaction when they'd been laying the roof yesterday.

"I swear he was so focused on that hornet I thought he was gonna step right off the house," Saul howled. "He just kept slowly backing up. I yelled his name three times before he finally took his eyes off that thing and realized what he was doing."

Mason laughed at himself right along with the rest of the crew even as he adamantly denied the claim.

"I was never gonna step off into thin air, leastways, not as long as the dang thing didn't land on me!" He said laughing loudly.

"He's always had the ability to keep his eye on the ball," Marshall spoke up in his baby brother's defense referencing Mason's glory days playing baseball.

"Come to think of it, Mason, and the rest of you fellows, too, you might be interested in joining me on the baseball field tomorrow night."

"What are you talking about?" Mason asked. "The only baseball going on these days is at the little league field when my boys play."

That's exactly where I mean," Marshall replied. "A few of us have been getting together on Thursday nights for a game. We're calling it the Old Timers League.

As the men burst out laughing Marshall continued, "well if the shoe fits, and in my case it does!" He said, laughing a little before continuing. "But I'm dead serious. It felt pretty good getting these rusty old bones moving again. We're having a good time with it. What's that they say? All work and no play. Well, anyway, I'd really love to see some of you fellows join in. So far we've only got enough players for two teams, with a bit more interest we can get some real competition going. You oughtta come on out tomorrow night and see what I'm talking about."

A few of them were talking about doing just that as they broke it up and headed back to work.

Marshall switched things up after lunch and spent the last part of the day working with Manny, Mitch and their crew. Working side by side he was keeping the personal touch going. It was a good chance to talk shop with his crew leader, too. Mitch and Marshall really didn't have much contact at work since Mitch was a crew member and Marshall was at Corporate the biggest part of the time. Marshall took the opportunity to team up with Mitch for a bit to touch base with him, too.

Thinking back over the day on his drive home that evening he was pleased with the end result. It had been both productive and pleasant. It was good to have an up close, personal and current feel for how the Hardee Street project was going.

CHAPTER 10

Checking the weather app on her phone Vonda chose a sleeveless, street length, flowered dress for this morning's church service.

Sunday's were her favorite day of the week. Thinking this over on her drive to church she realized she'd felt that way since childhood. Vonda's mother was in the habit of making a delicious dinner after church on Sunday's. There was always a lively conversation over the meal. Everyone then helped clear away the kitchen mess before each one retreated to their own rooms for an afternoon nap.

Her parents felt it was important to be refreshed for the new week. They always made sure Sunday was a restful day. Vonda seldom actually napped and at times wondered if anyone else in the family did either. It didn't really matter. Vonda just loved those afternoons. She enjoyed listening to music, reading, writing poetry or just lying on her bed daydreaming of the future, just enjoying the down time.

Sometimes her sister would venture into her room. They'd talk and laugh together as they filled each other in on whatever was going on in their lives. Thinking back now she realized there'd actually been many times she had curled up on her bed and rested for a bit before everyone gathered together again. She'd grown to love those relaxing Sunday's. That was proven true years later when she and Stanley were raising their own family. Vonda had kept her parents Sunday traditions alive.

During those Sunday afternoon meals, she was often impressed with Stanley's insight into scripture. They all talked about the morning's sermon often answering their older children's questions. Vonda had loved hearing the younger children sharing what they'd learned about God in their classes. They enjoyed showing everyone their crafts or colorings.

As the years passed and the children grew older some deep spiritual topics were covered. Those discussions sometimes even extended into and after the kitchen clean up. Finally, she and Stanley would retreat to their bedroom for some much-needed alone time after a busy week of working, running the household and taking care of their young family. Often times she'd curl up with her head on Stanley's chest as he'd watch a ball game. Vonda was still smiling from those happy memories when she arrived at the church she and Stanley had chosen together.

During the first three months of living in their new community they'd visited maybe six churches. They made note of the ones they liked well enough to return to. Those they visited several more times, all the while asking God to lead them. Then came a particular Sunday when she'd sat in this very service enjoying the music and how friendly the people were. Vonda loved how the scripture the Pastor used in the message so perfectly applied to her life. As she'd settled into the car for the ride home, she'd found herself thinking I'm really liking this church! She'd been asking God to lead them to a church that would be right for each of them individually as well as both of them together. Deciding to continue waiting for Stanley to tell her which church he felt drawn she'd said nothing.

After he pulled out of the church parking lot Stanley turned to her, smiled and said, "I really like this church, Vonda." It had been a perfect reminder that God works in mysterious ways. And just like that the decision was made.

This morning as Vonda sang along with her church family, she was overwhelmed by how beautifully all of their voices came together. Singing had always uplifted her heart and spirit. When the song ended, Pastor Mike stepped into the pulpit. He shared that Margie had asked to address the congregation. After thanking him for letting her speak Margie tearfully shared how much the church family had meant to her father who'd recently passed away. She thanked everyone for the many thoughtful things they'd done for him during his two-year battle with cancer.

Margie spoke of the many notes, visits, meals and other thoughtful things the people had done for him. Vonda knew exactly what she meant. She'd experienced the kindness of these people first-hand when Stanley passed away. They'd only been attending the church for three months and really hadn't gotten to know anyone very well. Vonda had been surprised then when so many reached out to her. Vonda thanked God for how He'd led them to just the right church. God knew Stanley would be going home soon and that these were the people Vonda would need during her grief. Everything they'd done for her then had gone a long way toward making this her church family now. Even now someone would always invite her to sit with them during services. People who recognized her from church would wave or stop for a chat when seeing her out and about in Logan.

As her focus came back to the present, she heard Margie mention that as many of them may already know her father owned the land adjoining the church property and the tired older building sitting on it. She shared that some of her happiest memories were of the years she worked there selling produce from his farm with her dad. She then surprised them all by telling them it was her dad's wish that the property be given to the church upon his passing. Pastor Mike stepped forward thanking her and telling her what an honor it was to have her father do this for the church family.

It was an exciting morning.

Driving home from church Vonda passed by the ball field and noticed there was a baseball game going on. Arriving at home she decided to go to the game. She quickly changed into jeans and a t-shirt and headed to the ball field.

CHAPTER 11

The little league Wombat team was playing against the Tigers. It was the bottom of the second inning when she arrived. A few spectators recognized Vonda and waved as she slipped into the stands. By the fourth inning the Wombats were leading 10-4 and Vonda was getting hungry.

There was quite a crowd at the concession stand but the line was moving pretty quickly so she joined in. While waiting to place her order, Vonda noticed two men from the Thursday night Old Timers League standing to her right talking together.

After paying for her food Vonda took a few seconds to balance the hot dog and fries in her left hand. Picking up her large soda with her right hand, she then turned to head back to bleachers. It was at that exact moment that one of the men she'd noticed earlier laughed loudly, slapped the other fellow on the shoulder and turned in her direction. His sudden movements startled her causing her to pull her upper body backward in an attempt to avoid him. Unable to keep it from happening she could only watch in horror as the soda in her right hand tipped forward. As he stepped into her pathway the soda cup fell forward. Soda poured out onto him at his shoulder and spilled all the way down his arm. Forgetting completely about the hot dog and fries in her right-hand Vonda threw that hand forward in an attempt to grab the soda. Of course, everything flew through the air and landed in a messy heap at their feet.

Completely stunned the man stood looking at her, his arm dripping of cold, wet, dark, sticky soda.

"Oh, I'm so sorry!" Vonda practically shouted as she began wiping his arm with her bare hands only managing to further smear the fizz of the soda into his skin.

Out of the corner of her eye she noticed the ketchup atop her white sneaker and all the food spread out at their feet. But none of that mattered. She felt absolutely terrible that he was drenched in soda. She quickly turned back toward the concession stand and grabbed the handful of napkins some kind stranger held out to her. Still apologizing, she quickly began dabbing at the soda soaked arm in front of her. It was then that his free hand gently covered hers stopping her movements.

"It's all right," his deep voice said as her eyes left his arm and traveled up to his face. Relief filled her as she saw him smiling.

"It's all right," he said again. "Don't trouble yourself. I'm fine! I'm a little wet and sticky but no harm done. Really! Please, let me help you get this mess cleaned up so the boys don't rush over here after the game and trample all over it!"

His laughter was genuine and relaxed but even more importantly it wasn't just coming from his mouth. It filled his eyes and spilled out from there.

Vonda liked him immediately.

She heard herself thanking him as they gathered up the messy food and carried it to the trash can nearby. Her attempt at getting that ketchup off her white sneaker only left a smeared shade of pink. After several attempts to clean it off she laughed and threw her hands up in the air.

"I'm Marshall," he said as he extended his sticky hand to shake hers.

"And I'm Vonda," she answered. "I truly can't apologize or thank you enough for helping me clear that mess away."

They chatted easily together as they walked over to the drinking fountain and took turns washing their hands and handing each other napkins to dry with. While walking back to the trash can to toss the wet napkins an excited young boy rushed between them, "Did you see my double play, Uncle Marshall," he asked excitedly before throwing his arms around the man's waist for a big hug?

"Sure did, buddy. That was something else!" Marshall answered as he gave Vonda a quick wink over the top of the boy's head.

CHAPTER 12

Victor had wanted an adventure and an adventure was exactly what he'd gotten. His calm life had quickly become a flurry of activity as he'd prepared to uproot from his Iowa home to plant himself in Stokesbury SC.

He gave the required two-week notice to his previous accounting firm during which time he sold everything of no sentimental value. This condensed his personal possessions to just what would fit in his vehicle. As it turned out there was very little that couldn't be replaced once he was settled.

It was with a very small amount of anxiety and a huge amount of excitement that he finally loaded his belongings, bid farewell to his family and hit the road headed for his adventurous new life.

He was especially happy with the townhouse he'd rented in downtown Stokesbury. Six very similar historic brick townhouses surrounded a circular courtyard area which was beautifully decorated with tropical trees and flowering plants. The designers had placed benches in various locations for the residents to utilize in socializing or for relaxing in quiet solitude, depending on their current mood. The living area of Victor's townhouse faced the courtyard. He found great pleasure in opening the blinds of the large picture window, allowing all of that natural beauty to greet him each morning.

It was equally enjoyable to observe the courtyard happenings as he went about his evening routine. The area took on a more subdued beauty as the shadows of dusk fell over the foliage each evening. Located directly above the living area his upstairs bedroom also faced the courtyard. Victor had placed a large, overstuffed chair near the window and always enjoyed a few moments of relaxed observation before closing his blinds and settling in for a good night of sleep.

The neighboring tenants were friendly yet nonintrusive. It wasn't long before he knew each of their names and felt comfortable enough to engage in a few moments of conversation.

On his first day with Davidson Construction Inc. he reported to Marshall's office. Marshall took him down the hallway to a small conference room where they met with two other gentlemen, Manny and Saul. The four men sat together around the table as Marshall, Manny and Saul shared their personal and business story. Marshall had started the company on his own.

33

He remained the sole owner. Due to their lifelong friendship and teamwork on various projects in their teen and young adult years they knew each other's skill level and work ethics. It only made sense for the three men to partner up, thus Manny and Saul had become partners. Along the way each of them had pursued and obtained higher education degrees to further benefit the company. Since Victor would be handling the finances as the firm's accountant and would obviously see everyone's pay, he was politely reminded this information was to remain confidential.

By the end of his first day Victor had been welcomed to the job by everyone from crew members on up. He had a great feeling about this company and was excited to begin what he believed would be a long and successful career there. As promised the former accountant had stayed on long enough to familiarize Victor with the location of all the needed forms and give him an extensive yet somehow vague outline of what needed done on a daily basis. Anxious to get on with his retirement he'd only stayed a few days and never fully explained the ordering of supplies, use of requisitions, or which specific vendors were regularly utilized.

After his predecessor left the company Victor honored his commitment to Mr. Davidson by doing extensive research on his own. He was quickly learning how best to handle the financial department of Davidson Construction. The Office Manager DeeDee was invaluable in the process. In fact, all of the existing staff was willing to be helpful.

At the end of this first month in his new location Victor was pleased to realize he'd experienced not one moment of regret over his decision to make such a huge life change.

By the end of his first year with the company Victor was feeling quite at home. Things were going so smoothly, in fact, that when his calendar reminded him, he'd been there almost a year it got him thinking.

Several days later as DeeDee was pouring her first cup of coffee Victor walked up to her with his coffee cup in hand.

"How about pouring mine?" he asked with a friendly smile.

"Certainly," she answered pouring the hot stream into his mug.

"I got to thinking, the other day, that since I'm coming up on one year here I might be ready to take some time off," he told her with a smile. "In fact, I jumped on the internet a few nights ago and started looking around. You know, I was an avid hiker back in Iowa."

Actually, she hadn't known.

"I've done quite a bit of hiking since my move here. There are some great hiking paths at the South Carolina State Parks and their absolutely beautiful. But mostly I've been going to the ocean. I've learned to snorkel. I've had a bit of fun trying jet skiing, parasailing and paddle boarding along with some ocean fishing from the piers. I got myself a Kayak and have been on the Waccamaw River in that a few times, too.

"Oh, I know," DeeDee answered with a smile. "It's not hard to pack a weekend around here."

"So, I got to thinking that with my adventurous move here going so well, I'm up for an equally adventurous vacation. Have you ever heard of Natures Adventure Trips?"

"Can't say that I have," DeeDee replied. What is it?"

"They're an adventurer's vacation resource I found online. I gotta tell you, I'm pretty pumped about it." He walked with her to her office.

"They've built their business on the premise that a nature get-away is the perfect vacation. Personally, I couldn't agree more!"

"Well, it sounds like you're narrowing down what you may want to do for your vacation," DeeDee said.

"You know it!" Victor went on to explain that he'd chosen the ten day adventure to Ecuador which included hiking, kayaking, cycling and snorkeling. The trip would have him hiking through the highlands kayaking over to the Galapagos Islands for snorkeling and cycling. Sightings of a variety of wildlife throughout the trip are guaranteed.

"It's the most adventurous thing I've ever done," Victor told her excitedly.

"If you've got the time let's take a look at the calendar and be sure this place can survive without me during the weeks I've chosen."

DeeDee pulled the Outlook Calendar up on her computer screen and they put their heads together over it. Victor explained his plan to return to Iowa to visit his family for a week after the tour.

Fifteen minutes later they were each satisfied the dates he'd chosen would work out perfectly and Victor could hardly wait to get home that evening so he could book his trip.

CHAPTER 13

Once she'd started attending the Old Timers ball games Thursdays quickly became Vonda's favorite weekday. Attending that game gave her something to look forward to all week and especially throughout the day on Thursday.

She supposed it was being an old timer herself that made her enjoy the games so much. The fun and banter taking place between the players reminded her there's fun to be had in every stage of life. It also reminded her of Stanley who was always ready with a witty comment and had so enjoyed life. He surely would have joined the team if they'd discovered these games together. While sitting in the stands watching and listening to the men, she could just imagine Stanley out there with them. Sometimes it made her heart a little sad that he wasn't the one on the pitcher's mound. He'd pitched in little league and all throughout high school.

One night she heard one of the men laughingly tell another fellow his legs just wouldn't run as fast as his mind was telling them to. Her heart immediately reacted. It was the exact type of comment Stanley would've made.

As the weeks passed, Vonda became more comfortable being an old Timers game spectator. She'd been able to put the spectators with the players and was getting to know the wives/girlfriends and children who attended. She'd often turn her head to smile at the family of a particular player when he made a good play as she joined them in cheering for him. She even found herself sitting with some of those families fairly often. The Old Timer games had quickly become a regular part of her life. They were helping her feel a part of this small community she and Stanly had chosen as their home.

Although pouring soda down a man's arm wasn't the best way to make a new friend, having met Marshall Davidson at his nephew's little league game had proven to be a blessing in disguise. It had been an eventful month since and Vonda couldn't help chuckling to herself while remembering the entire incident.

After his nephew Caleb's quick hug the two of them had stood together watching Caleb hurry back to the dugout. Marshall had then turned to Vonda taken her by the elbow and led her back toward the concession stand. He told her he was famished and insisted she allow him to replace her lunch. After all, it was his sudden turn in front of her that had caused their near collision and cost her the meal. Allowing him to be gallant Vonda refrained from arguing and thanked him profusely while waiting for their order. In truth, she had been looking forward to the meal and actually was famished. Returning to the bleachers Marshall had introduced Vonda to his youngest brother, Mason, whom she learned had an older son named Declan, along with Caleb, whom she'd just witnessed hugging his uncle. Once they were settled Vonda enjoyed her lunch and the lively conversation between the brothers while watching the Wombats beat the Tigers for a final score of eighteen to seven.

The following Thursday night found Vonda cheering for Marshall by name. Unbeknownst to her it made him secretly want to smile every time he heard her. He made sure to catch up with her when the game ended using the excuse of wanting to introduce her to his two childhood friends and business partners, Manny and Saul. They all stood around chatting for quite some time. Although the conversation was mostly lighthearted and fun, the interaction of the men revealed a real depth to the friendship they shared.

When everyone said goodnight and headed toward their respective vehicle Vonda noticed it was well past dusk. Feeling a bit hesitant to walk home alone Vonda offered to help Marshall and began gathering things up as they cleared the field together. She hoped he hadn't seen her trepidation but was thankful either way when he realized she was on foot and offered to give her a ride home. She'd been relieved to accept and realized she may have to rethink walking to the field if she was going to stay after the game was over.

Marshall walked her to the door making sure she was safe until she'd unlocked it. They politely wished each other goodnight. After thanking him again for the ride Vonda slipped inside. She immediately turned to her home security device ready to enter the code only to realize she'd forgotten to set it when she went out earlier. "Oh Vonda" she said to herself. "You're getting more forgetful all the time, old girl. It's a good thing you live in a safe neighborhood."

Going about her nightly routine she found herself feeling happier than usual. Her circle of acquaintances was expanding. For the first time since she'd lost Stanley she could honestly say Logan felt like home.

CHAPTER 14

Mason Davidson leaned back on the pine green leather couch in Dr. Helen Rossman's office.

It was his fourth personal therapy session with Dr. Rossman. In the first session he'd made a brokenhearted confession of an eye opening incident in which his wife, Stacey, had drawn back from him in fear. He'd never laid a hand on her. In all their years together he'd never laid a hand on her. He *would never* hurt her. But there it was in her recoil and in her eyes, *intense fear*. She actually thought he'd do her harm. His precious Stacey actually believed him capable of hurting her! *That absolutely broke his heart.*

Shortly after the incident they'd entered into a legal separation. After twenty years of marriage! Stacey assured him she loved him. She wanted to work things out. She just needed some space right now. He wasn't happy about it. He loved his wife and their two sons more than anything in this world. He didn't want to lose them. Yet, he'd seen the fear in her eyes. He knew it was real. You cannot trust someone you're afraid of. You cannot truly love someone you don't trust. And it makes it awfully hard to live with someone if you're afraid of them. He knew that. And so, out of desperation, he'd finally done what she'd been suggesting he do for years. He sought counseling.

Dr. Rossman came highly recommend for personal and family therapy. He told her that was why he'd chosen her, it was exactly what he needed, personal and then family therapy. He wanted to save his marriage. *Nothing else mattered.*

She'd asked about his family of origin.

His childhood was normal until his parents' unexpected death when he was fourteen. There was a quick transition as his oldest brother Marshall because legal guardian over him and his seventeen year old brother, Mitch. That wasn't without problems but he was sure that was to be expected. He'd known his wife, Stacey, since Jr. High but they didn't start dating until a year after graduation. They had only dated six months when Stacey told him she was pregnant. They loved each other so they quickly married. Stacey suffered a miscarriage the first week of their marriage. Since they hadn't told anyone they were pregnant they dealt with the loss privately and moved on. They spent several years getting to know each other in order to build a strong relationship before they brought a baby into it. Several years later they decided to have a baby but nothing happened. Years went by without a child. It was a difficult time for them. Finally, after a helpful medical procedure Stacey conceived and after ten years of marriage they were thrilled to welcome their oldest son, Declan into their lives. Three years later they had Caleb.

To end that first session Dr. Rossman asked him to consider what he perceived to be his issues. He was also to consider what he thought others in his life perceived as his issues. He was to return ready to discuss that in the second session, which he did.

To his thinking, Mason was easy going, fun loving, a diligent employee with good work ethic who for whatever reason, struggled to get along with others. He was a loving husband and father who, unfortunately, had a short fuse. It was Mason's belief that others perceived him as difficult to get along with and angry yet, also cheerful and fun loving at times.

He didn't understand their perception of him at all.

Dr. Rossman had then asked him point blank what exactly it was that he wanted from therapy. What he was willing to do to get it and how much introspection and personal examination he was willing to endure, despite how painful it may become. She was a straight shooter who didn't beat around the bush or coddle him. She'd explained, in no uncertain terms, that the road to good mental health usually wasn't easy. Sometimes it was downright brutal. The human mind is a powerful thing. It's been known to bury bad memories, hurtful truths and painful realizations in order to preserve its' own comfort. She'd given him a lot to think about when they ended the session.

In the third session Mason told Dr. Rossman he'd given it serious thought and he was committed to doing whatever it took to get to the bottom of his issues. He wanted to save his marriage but he also wanted to save himself. He didn't really know if he needed saving but he knew *something wasn't right*. It hadn't been right for as long as he could remember. He was tired. He was desperate and yes, he wanted to achieve what she called good mental health. He then shared that he'd had a lifetime of struggles he simply didn't understand.

And so they'd begun.

After some give and take between himself and Dr. Rossman he'd told her flat out that he didn't understand why - but could definitely see that he might have an underlying anger issue. In total frustration he stated "This makes no sense! I have a good job with my brother's company now. My wife loves me and I know we're going to work through all of this. I have absolutely nothing to be angry about!"

At that point Dr. Rossman was letting him take the lead in their sessions. She wanted him to feel safe enough to confide in her, which is an absolute necessity for therapy to be successful. As she'd previously explained to Mason the mind sometimes buries, hides or denies realities to protect people from hurtful emotions.

Once they began to delve into his life more extensively she was certain some deep seeded hurts were going to come to the surface. When that happened he would need to feel safe. He could only feel safe if he trusted her. By allowing him to choose which direction the topics of discussion went she was allowing him to open those tightly closed doors in the order in which he felt safest doing so.

CHAPTER 15

Although Victor had a pretty good handle on standard accounting practices when he joined the Davidson Construction team, he wasn't satisfied with his understanding of the details. He also needed to improve his vendor recognition in the area of construction supply purchasing.

The expansion of Davidson Construction Inc. had happened quickly and resulted in multiple construction projects in various locations. At that point, and since then, the selection of supply vendors had increased to the point of being quite extensive. It was a continuous frustration to Victor that a master list of current vendors had never been compiled. He had personally started that compilation on three separate occasions always to get side tracked before its completion.

After setting his vacation dates with DeeDee he'd decided to prioritize that particular project. His goal was to get the list completed by the time he went on vacation.

As invoice requisitions came across his desk he began adding the vendors name and contact information to an ever growing supplier list in his computer. He had to start somewhere and this seemed as good a place as any. Once he'd begun recording vendor names he naturally began glancing over the requisitions to be certain each particular vendor being used made it onto the list. He felt quite pleased each time he recognized a vendor and was able to confidently assure himself the vendor was already on the list. These instances were proof he was learning another area of his job, an area which he felt was of vital importance. Any time he didn't recognize a vendor's name he took the time to add the information to his list.

Over the course of several weeks Victor had noticed multiple requisitions coming through for a particular vendor. It made sense since the Hardee Street project was in full swing and all the supplies being ordered appeared to be for that project.

Upon closer scrutiny of a particular requisition it looked to Victor as if the supplies ordered had been listed twice. It struck him as odd that instead of listing a larger quantity of each item, the items had been relisted in the exact same order. It was a sizable order and while that was certainly a possibility for the Hardee Street project, it was strange the way the items had been listed. He wondered if perhaps a mistake had been made.

At the time he'd first noticed this Victor had laid the requisition aside until just such a time as this when he'd have an opportunity to invest time into researching the situation. A few moments later Victor was extremely perplexed after having called the phone number listed at the top of the requisition. After the phone rang several times he heard: "We're sorry - the number you dialed is not a working number. If you feel you've reached this recording in error, please hang up and try the number again." Victor did exactly that only to hear the same recording the second time. Several moments later the email he sent to the listed email address on the requisition came back as an undeliverable. Victor was now on Google maps trying to locate the actual business address. Oddly enough he was finding no listings for the business name that appeared on the requisition at all.

As his curiosity grew Victor decided to actively seek out the company file for this vendor. He wanted to satisfy his curiosity as to exactly how much business was being done with this vendor before he further investigated the situation.

When Victor was first hired DeeDee had showed him the filing cabinet containing active project files. She'd been very helpful in explaining the processing of the paperwork. The requisitions went through a series of steps from the time a supply requisition was completed to when it was filed after the payment had been made. Once the order was delivered the supply slip was submitted to accounting. After the accounting department made the payment the check cleared. At that point the requisition, along with the cancelled check was returned to DeeDee. Everything was then stapled together and filed in the individual vendor file. All completed requisitions were kept for the required seven years for auditing purposes.

On occasion Victor had needed to follow up on a particular payment so he was already familiar with the vendor file room. It was with great satisfaction that Victor was finally able to lay his hands on the file for the vendor in question. He returned to his office to familiarize himself with the vendor file and learn exactly how much business was being handled with this vendor.

It was with added frustration that Victor had to admit to himself, at the end of the hour, that he still hadn't really resolved anything.

He had, however, made a few discoveries. One being that every requisition in the file had been issued by one particular member of the Hardee Street project crew. Being as this was the first vendor file he'd actually examined in full he was uncertain whether this was an oddity or not. Perhaps it was company policy that one crew member place all the orders for each specific project. If so, this wouldn't be out of the ordinary at all. If not, it could be a bit concerning, especially in light of the fact that the contact information on each requisition was the exact same. This indicated that, contrary to what Victor had assumed, there hadn't been a business relocation which could've explained why the vendor contact information was leading nowhere. Being unable to locate the actual vendor organization or a contact person was becoming quite concerning.

Victor had gotten caught up in his research and it was late afternoon when he finally put the file away making a mental note to revisit that issue within the following work week.

CHAPTER 16

Unlike most Saturday's Vonda had an important event on her agenda today. Although she was stepping out of her comfort zone she was excited to do something helpful.

The property deed for the land Margie's dad had left to the church had recently been transferred over. Today was the first of several scheduled work days to convert that building to use for community and church gatherings. Vonda wasn't sure what she could do to help but had decided to participate. She was excited to lend a hand and perhaps become better acquainted with others in her church family.

It was no surprise to see a good number of people already hard at work when she arrived. A quick tour of the building revealed it was much larger than first glance would indicate. The back section, which had just been used for storage of farm equipment and produce, was to be converted to a kitchen. The front section would become a banquet area. The small bathroom was being extended and would be split into men's and women's restrooms. This facility would accommodate a good number of people and was going to be very nice once it was completed.

Today had been designated for planning, cleaning and basic repairs. Some of the men were busy making repairs and hammering could be heard throughout the building. Eager to help, Vonda set to cleaning the front windows. After years of neglect it was quite a task.

Almost two hours later, having finished all the windows, Vonda went to see where else she could be helpful. The other ladies had gotten the walls washed down and were finishing up by sweeping and mopping each individual room.

Vonda detoured through the back section of the building to see the overall progress as she made her way back to the church. Entering the large back room she saw Marshall Davidson quickly sketching in a pad as Pastor Mike described what he had in mind for the area. Vonda was surprised to see Marshall since he didn't attend her church. A few seconds later the two men finished the discussion and turned in her direction.

"Vonda!" Marshall exclaimed, a quick smile coming to his face.

"Oh, you two know each other?" Pastor Mike asked.

"We've only recently met," Marshall answered.

"Vonda's become part of our church family here," Pastor Mike said with a warm smile.

"Marshall's a member of our sister church over in Stokesbury," he said to Vonda. "He'll be heading up the construction of this renovation for us."

Vonda had often heard about the Stokesbury branch of Dogwood Alliance although she'd never actually been there. That church had been started by a former member who'd moved from Logan to Stokesbury years ago. The two churches often worked together, joined each other's congregations and helped with projects such as this one. This was the first time Vonda had been involved in any of the joint ventures.

"Oh, that's wonderful!" Vonda answered smiling warmly.

"We were just discussing the details of what we've got in mind," Pastor Mike added. Turning to include Marshall he said, "It's just about time for the catered meal to arrive. I hope you two have worked up an appetite."

"I know I have!" Marshall answered.

"I'm heading over to the church now to help get things set up," Vonda told them.

"I'll join you," Marshall said. "Perhaps they can use an extra set of hands."

And indeed they could. He was put to work setting up tables. Vonda and the other ladies were ready with tablecloths, tableware and utensils.

Once it was all in place and the food had arrived Marshall hurriedly returned to the renovation building to invite everyone to come and eat.

CHAPTER 17

Everyone was now gathered for the catered meal the church was providing for all those who'd come out for the first work day. Pastor Mike stood and thanked them all for coming and for the hard work they'd just put into the building. He then said a prayer thanking God for the donation of the land and building and asking that it be a blessing to everyone in the future. As soon as he said amen Marshall and Vonda got in line to get their meal.

While waiting Marshall asked her how long she'd been attending Dogwood Alliance Church. Vonda answered "two years" before sharing that almost three years ago her husband's job had unexpectedly closed. Since neither of them enjoyed the cold weather up north they'd always planned to retire to a warmer climate. With Stanley being forced to make a job change it just made sense to make the move instead of waiting. The Carolina's being centrally located between their grown children Stanley immediately began seeking work there. And they continued to pray for whatever would be best for their future.

Marshall and Vonda set their plates on the table and took seats directly opposite each other. Vonda said, "It wasn't long before everything started falling into place. When Stanley secured a position in Logan we put the house up for sale and made the move. Once we got settled we set about trying to find a good church."

Even after almost two years it wasn't easy for Vonda to talk about Stanley's death. She was a little surprised, then, at how comfortably she filled Marshall in on everything that had followed.

When she struggled with her emotions his eyes filled with compassion. Marshall was a very good listener. Vonda smiled as she told him how the people of this church had been there for her during her loss. She shared how the Grief Share program they offered was helpful for her that first year after she lost Stanley. She told him her very personal experience of how God had proven true to His promise never to leave us alone. And that Psalms 18:34 "The Lord is close to the brokenhearted and saves those who are crushed in spirit" had become her favorite verse of scripture through it all. She'd certainly felt crushed in spirit in those first months after losing Stanley. How wonderful it was to realize that before she'd even known she was going to need them God had surrounded her with people who would truly care for her.

To her own surprise she then admitted to still feeling a bit isolated in Logan outside of her church connections. She explained that having been the motivating factor behind her recent attendance at games on the baseball field. Marshall smiled and told her how glad he was for that adding that he was enjoying their new friendship.

Picking the conversation up at that point Marshall shared having been born and raised in Stokesbury. His parents were wonderful, loving people. His father and the man who started the Alliance church in Stokesbury had been friends for years. That man was instrumental in his parents coming to faith in Christ and getting involved in the church. His parents later had a hand in starting the outreach that now provides food for those in need. Marshall had become a Christ follower during Jr. High and went on to become a leader among the youth. He worked closely with his father on many church projects, house repairs and renovations for senior citizens while growing up. This not only gave him the skills needed to land a job on a construction crew during high school but also a compassion for the elderly and a deep seeded desire to help others.

What he didn't know about construction work he quickly learned on the job. He got his own apartment soon after graduation. Already envisioning owning his own company he devoted most of his time to work and furthering his education. After obtaining his college degree in business management he quickly became a crew leader. He was twenty five and working toward his career goals when his parents were suddenly and tragically killed in a car accident. He had leaned heavily on his best friends, Manny and Saul, during that time. His brother Mitch had just turned seventeen and Mason was fourteen. Marshall stepped in to become their legal guardian and set about to complete the job of raising them. Of course, it was a daunting task that took all of his time and energy outside of work.

"Mitch has always been a bit like our mother," he told Vonda. "I see her quiet spirit in him. With his thick, dark hair and the set of his eyes he even looks like her. But more than that, like her, he's an introvert. Quiet and reserved. It wasn't easy to know what he was feeling after the death of our parents, though truthfully I didn't delve into that with either of the boys. Mitch has always been responsible and hardworking. He didn't give me any trouble during the two years he lived with me before going out on his own. He got a job that summer and continued working after school during his Sr.

year. He worked with several companies over the years before he eventually became a member of my construction crew. He's remained a bachelor and has done fairly well for himself financially from what I can see. He's always driven a very nice vehicle. Right now he actually has two. He bought a home in an upscale area of Stokesbury a few years back. He's never really had a steady girlfriend that I've seen. Although over the past few years it seems he's mentioned the same one whenever it's come up, so maybe there's more there than I'm seeing." Marshall smiled and continued. "I'm happy he's doing so well. In those early years it seemed as if he went out of his way to make things easier for me. Believe me, I needed that, especially since Mason took every bit of energy I had and then some. While his quiet nature was helpful at the time I've sometimes wondered how Mitch really dealt with our parents' death. I've never really talked about that with either of the boys."

Vonda noted that even though all three men were well into their forty's now Marshall often referred to his brothers as "the boys". She found it endearing.

"It took everything I had just to be sure their basic needs were met and they completed their education," Marshall continued. "I had no experience dealing with the fallout of death and knew very little about grief. Truthfully, I'm not even sure I ever grieved our parents properly myself. I already had a lot on my plate. I got the boys pretty quickly and it was off to the races trying to get everything done and keep my sanity.

Whether it was grief of just teenage rebellion, Mason didn't make things easy in the four years he lived with me. It seemed to me he was angry most of the time and he became more argumentative each day. I assumed he was angry that they'd died and left us. Truthfully though, he may've already been that way. I'd been out of the house for several years by that time and was busy building my career. I really didn't know my brothers very well when it all happened. Mom and dad could've been having trouble with Mason already. I have no idea. All I can tell you is that Mason was a handful. He had an attitude that wouldn't quit."

Watching his face as he spoke it amazed Vonda how she could literally see the stress as it crept into his features and settled in as he spoke. Her heart went out to him as she imagined such a young man bearing such huge responsibilities.

He sighed heavily and continued, "I was constantly being called to the school due to his fighting. It was exhausting. He started skipping classes and his grades were failing. I never knew where he went or what he was doing. It was a time, I tell ya. I wasn't sure he was even going to graduate. That was a worry, for sure. I had no idea how he was going to make it in life without a diploma. I had several serious conversations with him about that. It must've helped because he did manage to pull through. I was so relieved the day he graduated! He didn't try to stay with me after that, but he did continue to struggle. Most of his adult life he's gone from job to job." He looked away thoughtfully before adding, "I guess some of us just have a harder time growing up than others."

Marshall paused a moment before continuing, "I did the best I could by both of them. Looking back now, I'm sure it would've been better if we had been in church. It would've built faith into our lives. I've sure come to rely on my own faith through the years. I'm not a firm believer that organized church is always the answer. But I don't know where I'd be without my relationship with Christ. He's the one I depend on when there's nothing else *I can* depend on. I don't know how folks make it through the hard times without faith and there's no joy like the joy of knowing God loves us just as we are. But still, if I'd had us in church back then we'd have had the support of a church family. I'm sure it would've been easier. But, like I said, I wasn't going myself at the time. Then once I took my brothers in it was just too much to even think about. I had so much going on already. Neither of them ever asked about it so I was willing to let it fall away. It's troublesome for me now, I'll admit. There's no evidence of faith in either of their lives. Truthfully, it seems as if I failed them in that area. My parents would be disappointed, I'm sure."

It had been years since Marshall had talked about any of this with anyone. He had no idea what had possessed him to share it all with Vonda but she'd been an excellent listener. He met her eyes now and saw nothing but compassion and tenderness looking back at him.

"I can relate to so much of what you've shared with me," she said quietly. "We experienced some of what you've been through when we were raising our children. Just as you were saying about your brothers - each child is so different. It's not like one thing works with all of them. It's hard to know the best approach to take sometimes. I imagine it was much more challenging for you, since they were your brothers and not your own children. Also, you were doing it alone. As you mentioned, you hadn't even been raising them up until that point. No doubt the grief of losing your parents compounded everything. My heart really goes out to all three of you. I'm not sure how that part works, of course, but I really believe your parents know you did the best you could. I imagine they're *so very proud of you.*"

If he hadn't meant it before he certainly meant now what he had said earlier about enjoying their new friendship. She was so easy to talk to and so kind. As they began to clear their mess away, Vonda reached over and laid a hand gently on his. When he looked up she met his eyes and said, "I'm going to be praying for you and your brothers, Marshall. I have a feeling God's not done with any of you yet."

He was deeply touched, more deeply touched than he had been in a very long time. "That's the best thing anyone can do for us." He answered. "*Thank you, Vonda.*"

CHAPTER 18
THAT FATAL DAY

Starting out this morning he had no idea today would be a turning point in his life.

The new house on Hardee Street was almost done. They were going over everything to tie up loose ends and moving the big equipment to the lot next door where another new residence would soon be built. There was some random clean up that still needed done when the shift ended. He told the other guys to head on out and he'd wrap things up. He then finished the outside and worked inside for over an hour. He was just about finished when Victor startled him. He'd come in quietly, walked up behind him and then suddenly asked for a moment of his time.

He turned immediately to give Victor his full attention. Victor seemed a bit nervous as he lifted his briefcase and placed it on the countertop. Talking the entire time but not really making sense. He was stumbling over his sentences. Finally, he lifted a large handful of papers and held them up.

"I'm not sure how to say this but to just come right out with it. Is this company even real?"

Feeling his face grow hot he simultaneously had the sensation that the blood in his entire body was draining toward his feet when he looked Victor in the eyes. He'd been caught off guard. More to the point; *he'd just been caught*.

He'd never expected this moment to actually arrive. Somehow, he had come to believe *he'd never get caught*. He'd been getting away with it for *so long* that it just seemed like there was no risk anymore. But now it was happening. He was being confronted and he had *no idea* how to handle it. Adlibbing the best he could he took an angry stance, raised his voice aggressively and reacted, "What are you talking about? Is what real? What company? Uh, you seem to be holding a stack of supply requisitions for some company you don't think is real. I'd say it must be real with all those orders, wouldn't you?!"

"I'd *like* to say so. But oddly enough, despite all the information on these requisitions I can't seem to locate an actual company," Victor offered.

Still maintaining the aggressive voice he responded with, "Well, I don't know why you're asking *me* about it! It's not like *I* own the place."

Victor wasn't backing down. In fact, his voice seemed to be escalating to match the attitude he was being given.

"As far as I've been able to determine you're the *only* crew member who's *ever* placed an order using these requisitions. It appears you're *the only person* at Davidson Construction who has ordered from *this* particular vendor *at all*. I haven't gone any further with this. I came to you first - I came to you out of respect but I'm beginning to rethink that as I'm sure not getting any respect in return."

He could feel the panic continuing to rise up inside him. His heart was pounding. His blood was racing. His face was growing warm. Not knowing what else to do he continued to go with what he'd started. He heard his voice escalating as he said he didn't know anything about being the only one using those requisitions. He was placing orders just like the rest of the guys. He was doing his job just like everyone else and he didn't appreciate being accused of, whatever this was. He didn't even know *what* he was being accused of!

Victor's tone matched his own. As he began waving the papers clenched in his fist higher in the air and again demanded. "Just answer the question. *Is this company even real?*"

Caught up in the moment and blinded by fear he was disguising as anger he shouted, "How am I supposed to know? Who do you think I am? What are you *even saying*?" As the panic overtook him he rushed toward Victor reaching for the papers and shouting, "I have no idea what you're even talking about! Let me see those!"

Instinctively, Victor raised the clenched fist full of papers even further above them and took several steps backward. Losing his footing suddenly he went straight down in a backward fall. Victors head struck the kitchen island directly behind him and in the next instant he lay motionless on the floor.

Not realizing Victor had hit his head he rushed forward still ranting. Seeing that Victor wasn't moving he shouted, "Oh, just get up, Victor! This isn't over! Not by a long shot!" You wanna accuse me of something? Then come on. Right here, right now. You might as well just come right out and say it!"

Staring down at Victor's still form his mind slowly registered the odd angle at which Victors head lay away from his body. After only about three seconds clarity began to set in. It didn't look natural. Only then did he realize

Victors eyes were wide open but strangely appeared unseeing. They were staring straight ahead and unmoving.

"Victor?" His voice grew quiet. "Victor? Come on man. Can you hear me?"

A new form of panic began to replace the panicked anger of mere seconds before. "No, Victor. *No.* Come on now, buddy, answer me. Get up. We'll straighten this out. *Victor, come on!*"

The truth was quickly making itself clear. Victor wasn't getting up. He wasn't going to answer. Victor Tonnae was *never getting up again.* His eyes were dead. His body was lifeless.

Falling to his knees in shock he buried his face in his hands and softly moaned.

It took just short of ten minutes for him to pull himself together.

As reality settled in he finally checked Victor to see if he was breathing. He then checked for a pulse. Finding neither he was forced to face the truth. Accepting it had taken a bit longer. But after acceptance mere seconds passed before he'd began working things out in his mind.

He was now taking the needed actions.

There was no logical reason for anyone from the crew to return tonight, but just in case, he moved Victor's body to a closet.

Glancing around to be sure nothing looked unusual he turned all the lights off. Looking out the front window and seeing no one he walked out and got into his truck. Quickly and quietly he drove to the back of the property and parked at the edge of the woods. He'd taken Victor's car keys and cell phone from his pockets and the wad of requisitions from his hand. He'd torn those to shreds and would dispose of all of those items separately along the way. A quick but thorough search of the brief case assured him no other requisitions would be found. Still seeing no one about he'd pulled his baseball cap low over his face, walked out, got into Victor's car and drove away. Thinking quickly he grabbed the sunglasses off the visor and put them on. It wouldn't do to be recognized if he happened to pass anyone who might know him, especially once he reached Stokesbury.

Half an hour later he turned onto Bailey Street not far from West Pine and saw an open spot ahead. Perfect! He parallel parked and used the shop cloth he'd had the good sense to grab from the house to quickly wipe down the steering wheel, door handle, brief case and everything else he may've touched inside the car. Exiting the car he hit the lock, discreetly wiped down the door handle, kept his head down and casually walked away. He headed east toward the city transit bus stop a short two blocks ahead. This was one of the reasons he'd chosen to bring the car here. He'd known he could take the bus back to Logan. The other reason was the Grey Hound bus station that was two blocks in the opposite direction. Whenever the car was found it could easily be assumed Victor had skipped town on a bus. It wasn't a perfect plan but it wasn't bad either. He'd always been a quick thinker.

Less than an hour later he hopped off the bus at Food Lion on West Main in Logan. Just to make it look good he immediately headed into the grocery store. If the bus driver was questioned at some later date, he'd report having seen him go into the store.

Five minutes later he left the store and made his way over to the side street. Under cover of darkness he wound around a bit, although he was actually quite confident no one was watching him. He slipped into the woods that backed up to the new house and made his way back.

Now to deal with the body...

CHAPTER 19

Mason felt tired, mentally and physically tired. Unconsciously, he leaned back and allowed himself to sink into the cushion of the therapy office couch. Almost immediately Dr. Rossman entered the room.

She was carrying a small container which she set down on the table in front of him. She then proceeded to lay round chips in a variety of colors onto the table. There were five chips of each color; Black, Red, Yellow, Blue, White, Green, Orange, Grey and Purple. Beside each color she placed a small white card with the name of an emotion written on it. It went like this; Black - Depressed, Red - Angry, Yellow - Cheerful, Blue - Subdued, White - Calm, Green - Envious, Orange - Energetic, Grey - Tired, Purple - Frustrated.

Dr. Rossman sat in the straight back chair she always sat in across from him. She told Mason she wanted to do something a little different over the next several sessions. She then pointed to the table.

"These will be lying on the table when you arrive for your next session. I'd like you to think back over the week. I'd like you to pick up the chips that represent the emotions you experienced throughout the week. You may take as many of each chip as you feel it takes to represent the amount of each emotion you experienced. For example how are you feeling right now?"

Without hesitation Mason replied, "Tired".

"Excellent," Dr. Rossman responded. "Please pick up the amount of Grey chips you feel represent how tired you're feeling right now."

Mason leaned forward and picked up 3 of the grey chips. He then studied the table for a moment and proceeded to pick up 1 blue chip and 1 black chip.

Dr. Rossman smiled.

"Very good, Mason. In fact, that's excellent. That's very helpful. You're telling me you're very tired tonight. You're also feeling a little depressed and a bit subdued. Is that correct?"

"You got it, Doc," Mason answered with a half-smile. He was enjoying this game.

Mason had grown fairly comfortable with Dr. Rossman over the past four weeks. She was a straight shooter and he liked that in a person.

"Okay, good," she said. "Now let's take this a little bit further. I'd like you to take a moment and think back over this past week. I want you to remember events and instances, just whatever stands out in your mind. Next I want you to identify the emotions that were evoked in each case. Once you've done that pick up the chips that represent your feelings."

Mason did as she'd asked. They then spent the next several minutes talking about the emotions he'd experienced and what had provoked them in each instance. After they had completed the exercise Dr. Rossman reminded him they'd be doing this each week when he arrived for his sessions. She had him replace the chips and they began to revisit his last session.

Picking up where they'd left off Mason went on to tell Dr. Rossman the extensive history of his jobs. They delved into the fact that despite being a dedicated and hard worker with excellent work ethic Mason had frequently been let go. Mason gave her detailed explanations of what had happened and been said in many of the instances. Some employers' sugar coated things by telling him they just didn't have as much extra work as they'd expected so there was no longer a need for his position. Most of the time he didn't buy that and more times than not he later learned he'd quickly been replaced. A few of the employers came right out and told him what the real problem was. In those instances it was always a matter of Mason's attitude or of his co-workers having interpreted his behavior or speech as aggressive. After a significant amount of back and forth dialogue they established that it seemed that most employers didn't see him as a good fit with other workers. Once again Mason found himself feeling frustrated. This wasn't how he perceived himself at all, nor was it how he wanted others to see him.

CHAPTER 20

Driving onto the church property the morning after the first Saturday work day Vonda looked over at the building. The clean windows brought a smile to her face. The building and the grounds around it looked so much better.

Entering the sanctuary always felt like coming home again. Being greeted with hugs and handshakes was so heartwarming. She loved to sit chatting happily with several of the other ladies until the service began.

The first congregational song flowed over her soul like a soothing mountain stream. Pastor Mike shared the success of the previous day's work and gave a brief overview of the changes to come. Vonda felt especially pleased she'd chosen to participate. At Pastor Mike's invitation several stood and shared what being part of the work day had meant to them. Everything was uplifting and positive so it made no sense when Vonda felt a rising sense of sadness deep inside.

Thinking about that later in the afternoon, she supposed it was because Stanley wasn't here to help. He had always been the first to help with church and community projects. When they moved to Logan he'd been insistent these were the opportunities that would help him feel at home and bond with the men in their new church.

When Pastor Mike began his message Vonda felt as if God was speaking right to her heart. The sermon was taken from Isaiah 43:18-19 "Forget the former things; do not dwell on the past. See, I am doing a new thing! Now it springs up; do you not perceive it? I am making a way in the wilderness and streams in the wasteland."

The application was, or course, to the donated building and how it had wasted away for years but God was now giving it a new purpose. God was about to do new things with that old building. Vonda loved how scripture, though thousands of years old, could so often be applied to current life. As she read over those words she was reminded that no matter what has taken place in our past God can do something new with us *if only we'll let Him.*

Stanley kept coming to mind and with him there arose that twinge of sadness. Driving home she talked it over with God. As she'd often done during the past two years she talked with Him about how hard life was without Stanley. Vonda had never been one to mince words with God so she spoke quite honestly about how she was feeling. After all, she thought, He knows our every thought already. He loves us and wants us to tell Him our every hurt and our every joy exactly the way David did in the Psalms. As a new believer, many years before, Vonda had read through the Psalms. It was where she'd learned that God is there for us always. He promises never to leave us or forsake us and He never does!

Still feeling a little out of sorts Vonda had chosen to relax after lunch by watching a few old home videos. Sometimes it was fun to revisit the past. She'd laughed 'til she almost cried watching the kids ride that old go cart Stanley had found at a flea market and brought home for them. What fun they'd all had. That sure lifted her spirits.

As evening approached, Vonda found herself analyzing the sadness she'd been feeling for most of the day. She realized grief was overshadowing her again. If there was one thing she'd learned since she lost Stanley it was that grief has a mind of its own. At times it just seems to come out of nowhere and for no particular reason. There's no way of knowing how long it'll last and there's nothing you can do but ride the wave. Looking back now Vonda was very thankful she'd attended Grief Share group. It had helped her then and it was still helping her now. What she learned about grief then caused her to recognize what was happening now. She was being hit by another wave.

At the time of the loss grief is overwhelming, like a huge ocean wave that's knocked you over. You may even feel like you're in a fog for months. Eventually, though, you no longer feel like you're under water. As you're able to take tiny steps forward you begin to get your bearings. You gain ground. But another wave of grief can hit at *any time.* Vonda had been doing well for the past several months but here it was again - another wave.

Vonda had learned during her lifetime that happiness often starts with contentment. She was trying to be content with where life had taken her. But she'd be lying if she denied missing Stanley and the life they had shared. These were her thoughts and struggles as she went to bed on Sunday night.

On Monday there was an unexpected problem at the house. A problem Stanley would've handled. As the sole homeowner now she'd spent the day dealing with it. It felt very unfair and added to her overwhelming sadness. These were the times she needed Stanley. But he wasn't here. So Vonda cried.

On Tuesday she stumbled across one of Stanley's favorite TV movies. She immediately stopped everything, curled up on the couch and spent the next two hours watching it. She remembered watching it with Stanley which brought back how much she missed him. And again, she cried.

Wednesday was a pretty good day.

CHAPTER 21

While walking back to the house, he played over in his mind everything he had done since leaving in Victor's car. Mentally going down a checklist until he was certain he'd thought of everything. There was nothing left to do now but to get rid of Victor's body.

The timing of this couldn't have been better. By pure coincidence or just plain dumb luck the cement truck was due first thing tomorrow morning to lay the driveway for the house. The new house they'd just completed on Hardee Street, the house in which Victor had died earlier this evening.

All he had to do was bury the body, smooth the ground over it and no one would be the wiser. Victor's body would be gone leaving nothing to trace back to him. He could then put this ugly business behind him and go on with his life.

The difficulty was that everything had to be done under cover of darkness. As luck would have it there was a three quarter moon tonight so the sky wasn't totally dark. The completed house was the furthest one from the existing occupied residences. Any activity near it, especially at this hour, would surely go unnoticed.

Thankfully, he'd taken to keeping a change of clothes in his truck for just this type of occasion. Well, *not exactly this type of occasion*. It was for occasionally being detained at the work site longer than expected with no time to return home for clean clothing before an evening out.

Arriving back at the house he quietly retrieved his gym bag from the seat of his truck, carried it in and dropped it on the floor. Opening it he was relieved to see a black turtleneck atop clean jeans. He pulled the shirt on over his white t-shirt.

Walking as quietly as possible despite the fact that the house was totally empty but for him and Victor's body he hoisted the body up from the closet floor and carried it to the kitchen. He laid it down just inside the garage door.

With no intention of entering the house again once this was done he did a once through to be sure all he'd needed to do earlier was done. He then made sure nothing would indicate that Victor had ever been here. Finally, he retrieved his gym bag and left it in easy reach of the door.

Stepping into the darkened garage and over to the corner where the crew always piled their tools he slid his finger upward across his cell phone screen.

Seeing the icon for flashlight he touched it. Using the tiny light beam he located a shovel and headed for the side door of the garage. Extinguishing the flashlight beam just before stepping out into the yard he covered the six foot distance to the front of the garage and walked out onto the driveway. Along the edge of the driveway and close to the house he began to dig. The hole only had to be deep enough to lay Victor's body down and cover it with ten inches of dirt.

The cement truck would arrive in the morning. The driver would back up to the edge of the driveway and begin pouring onto the prepared area. As long as he got the body completely covered and the dirt smoothed out to the same height as the dirt around it nothing would appear amiss.

He worked quietly, quickly and steadily. The sooner he got this done the sooner he could walk away putting this entire event behind him forever.

He'd been in the construction industry long enough to have estimating sizes down to an exact science. Victor was about five foot eight inches tall. When he had the hole dug to an estimated size of two foot by six foot he stopped digging.

Looking around intently, he saw no car lights approaching. He did notice a soft glow coming from the nearest house which was still a good four vacant lots away. He supposed it to be a table light left on all night by the homeowner. He remembered noticing that same glow a few other times when he'd been to this job site after dark.

He dropped the shovel onto the ground and retraced his steps into the kitchen where he hoisted Victor's body up and carried it outside. He purposely avoided looking at Victor's face as he positioned him in the shallow grave and covered him with the discarded dirt.

He didn't let himself think about what he was actually doing. Instead, he concentrated on getting the dirt smoothed out so nothing looked out of place once the body was completely covered.

He then made sure to smooth out the area where he'd piled the dirt while digging earlier. When the job was completed he went back into the garage and found a yard rake. He raked the entire driveway area smooth so that none of the surrounding ground looked different from the rest.

When he was certain no one would be the wiser he gathered his gym bag, locked the door to the house and closed it behind him. He then headed to the back side of the house to where he'd moved his truck earlier so no one would realize he was still there.

Without the head lights he turned on the engine and put the truck into gear. He quietly coasted off the property, onto the dirt road, up to the curve in the road and around the corner. Feeling the pavement beneath him, at last, he breathed a sigh of relief. After he took the last turn onto the next road he turned on his headlights and let out the breath he hadn't even realized he'd been holding and headed home.

Each mile took him closer to home and with each one he felt just a bit more tension slip out of his body. Once there he undressed and showered. He then gathered his clothing and loaded the washing machine with everything he'd been wearing at the job site and while dealing with Victor's body. While the clothes washed and dried he methodically went through his memory checking off everything he'd done this evening to be sure nothing had been overlooked.

When the dryer buzzer sounded he folded and hung each item, putting everything away neatly. He was counting on everything being dealt with this night so there'd be nothing to remind him of what he'd just done when he woke up in the morning.

As much as he wanted to be there to watch the cement being laid for the driveway he wasn't on the schedule until one o'clock the next afternoon. Arriving early would be noticed and questioned. It was better to stick to the schedule.

Being part of a construction crew he was used to hard physical labor. Still, the last thing he noticed before drifting off to sleep was the ache in his shoulders. Apparently, the tension involved in burying a man wasn't quite what his body was used to. He sure hoped this would be the last time he'd have to think about that.

CHAPTER 22

It had been a rough week for Vonda. A wave of grief had hit her on Sunday and she'd cried at least once every day except for Wednesday. It was now Thursday and wasn't looking to be as good. From the time she woke up she felt quite depressed. She didn't even get dressed and found herself crying before noon. Totally unmotivated, she then spent most of the day in her recliner with the TV on but, truthfully, she'd slept more than anything else.

That evening she made herself eat a sandwich and a little soup. Knowing she needed to snap out of it she pushed herself into walking over to the ball field even though she still felt like crying. Once there she was faced with the prevailing feeling that this was something Stanley would have loved which just made her want to cry again. There were a few smiles, waves and goodnight wishes but other than that, as if sensing her needs, the others left her alone. Marshall waved in her direction and smiled but was tied up talking with Manny and Saul after the game. Walking home alone her heart was heavy. She was so despondent she wasn't aware of anything going on around her. She felt as if she was surrounded by a grey cloud.

"Help me, Father," she prayed in desperation. "Please help me get through this wave of grief that's washing over me. I feel like I'm drowning. Without you, I'm not sure I can get out of it this time."

When she was almost home she looked up and saw her house as she was approaching it. It was such a lovely home in such a good area of town. She and Stanley had felt so blessed to get a move-in ready home after all the fixer uppers they'd looked at. They were trying to buy within a certain price range since this was to be their retirement residence. When they realized this house was only two years old they decided to spend a bit more and forego all the renovations of an older home. It didn't take them long to realize it was one of the best decisions they'd ever made! Vonda couldn't help thinking that was especially true considering how it had all played out. God knew Vonda was going to be alone soon after they moved in. If they'd bought a fixer upper she'd have been left with projects she couldn't deal with on her own. Instead, here she was with this comfortable, beautiful house to go home to.

"I'm so very blessed," Vonda said aloud. She continued in her heart and mind, talking with God as if He were walking along beside her. I have so much to be thankful for, Lord. I don't want you to think I've forgotten how you've helped me and how far I've come since Stanley left me and joined you. Thank you for that and for my lovely home. Your word promises that I can do anything through Christ who gives me strength. I know you'll keep giving me what I need to get through each day, find my new normal and have joy in my life.

Entering her home she was greeted by Lilly's soft meowing. Vonda made a cup of hot tea and curled up in her recliner and turned on the TV. Lilly gently leapt into the chair and curled up beside her. Before long they were both asleep.

It was well after ten when Vonda woke up. Having slept a lot earlier in the day she wasn't tired enough for bed so she got her most recent book out and read a while. By midnight she was tired of reading but still not tired enough to sleep. She laid the book aside and sat quietly looking around the room. Only then did she realize she'd left the window blinds open when she'd dozed off earlier. She usually didn't like the window treatments open after dark, but tonight she enjoying looking out over the darkness beyond her window. It wasn't long before she noticed a strange recurring flash of light over by the Hardee Street house. There it was again. Ok, there. What was that? Her curiosity got the best of her and she gently put Lilly down and walked over to the sliders. Silently, she turned the bar for the full length window blinds so that the entire row inched backwards. Once there was enough space for her to step outside she opened the slider and stood looking intently toward the new house. She could still see the flash of light every fifteen seconds or so. It was fairly close to the ground. What was that? In the quiet of the night she realized she was also hearing repetitive scraping and clunking sounds now that she was outside. The sounds and the light were both repetitive though not quite in sync with each other. This was definitely a mystery. She was very focused as she tried to solve it. Three or four minutes later she realized the sounds had stopped. A few more seconds told her the light was gone now, too. After waiting silently for one more minute without the sound or the light returning she stepped back inside the sliders and locked them in place. Whatever was happening had stopped. She stood looking over at the new house for a few more minutes.

It was a beautiful night and the stars seemed especially bright. She thought there might be a full moon but looking up she saw it was only three quarters. Still it was a beautiful moonlit night so she stood enjoying it for maybe five more minutes. Glancing back over at the new house one last time she saw nothing usual. As she reached over to draw the blinds shut a reflection on the dirt road at the back of her property caught her attention. She turned toward it and realized there was a truck driving up the road with no headlights on. How strange was that? She watched until it turned off onto the next road. Just before it drove out of sight she saw the headlights come on. She found herself thanking God that the driver had turned his lights on. She asked God to watch over that vehicle and get him home safely since something obviously wasn't quite right.

Vonda was finally feeling a bit tired but didn't want to be alone in the bed so she turned back toward her living area. Settling into her recliner again she softly called Lilly who obliged with a gentle leap up into her lap. Vonda covered herself up and Lilly spent a few minutes kneading the throw cover before curling up comfortably as they both settled in to get some rest.

CHAPTER 23

Entering Dr. Rossman office Mason saw the colored chips lying on the table. He immediately thought back over the past week and identified emotions evoked as he remembered specific events and instances. He'd enjoyed this game the first time he'd played it. Now? *Not so much.*

With each passing week he'd found himself picking up purple chips representing his frustrations as well as red chips representing his anger. He didn't like that at all. He soon sat again staring at the chips in front of him and wrestling with his emotions. Finally, he picked up some chips, laid them in a pile in front of him and looked at Dr. Rossman.

Her left eyebrow rose slightly but she didn't say anything. As they'd been doing each week she asked him to identify the emotions evoked and share a few details of the events that evoked them.

Mason picked up the blue chip and told her he'd woken up without much energy one morning. He felt subdued most of that day. She accepted that and they moved on. He picked up the yellow and orange chips and smiled as he told her about having his sons, Declan and Caleb, with him over the weekend. He felt cheerful and energetic as he usually did when they spent time together. They'd gone hiking and tossed the baseball around a bit. Mason went through the rest of the chips he'd chosen fairly quickly. When he stopped talking Dr. Rossman sat quietly just looking at him. He hadn't picked up a purple or red chip at all today. Dr. Rossman wasn't saying anything. She was just sitting quietly looking at him.

He was feeling frustration through his entire body.

Finally, she spoke. "Okay Mason, is that it then?"

Mason felt very uncomfortable. He looked her dead in the eyes but didn't answer.

Dr. Rossman continued to sit quietly in her chair as another moment went slowly by.

"We've covered all the emotions you felt this week then? We can move on?" she finally asked.

Mason looked directly at her again but still didn't answer. She sat calmly, just waiting. Another moment began to drag by and with each passing second he could feel the frustration and anger building inside him.

Suddenly he reached across the table and grabbed the purple chips.

"There! Are you happy now?" he shouted angrily. "I feel frustrated right now." Grabbing some red chips violently he shouted, "Yes! I felt angry this week! Is that what you're waiting for? Are you happy now?!"

Dr. Rossman very calmly leaned forward in her chair. She looked him in the eye and gently said, "No, Mason. I'm not happy now. I'm sorry you're struggling with these emotions. I'm trying to help you identify them. I'm trying to help you dig deep so we can find out where they're coming from. I'm trying to help you face them. Until you can face them we can't resolve your issues."

Mason felt spent.

He wanted to cry.

But instead he just sat there looking at her.

Dr. Rossman was good at what she did. Still he wasn't sure she could really help him. They'd been at this for weeks. And yes, he was finally able to verbalize his frustrations. Yes, he was beginning to recognize that he did feel an underlying anger most of the time. But he still didn't understand why.

As if she could hear his thoughts Dr. Rossman quietly began to speak. She calmly reiterated what he'd just been thinking. She told him that the purpose of what they'd been doing with the chips over the past several weeks had been to help him identify emotions in everyday life events. She explained that sometimes due to the things we experienced in our upbringing, traumatic situations, abusive relationships, grief, and any number of other factors our brain learns to mislabel our emotions. Sometimes it even learns to shut them down completely. It does these things in an effort to help us avoid pain.

Her voice was having a calming effect on him and he gave in to it.

He felt the anger subsiding as he listened. She reminded him of what she'd told him in their first session. That the brain is a powerful source and will sometimes go to great lengths to protect us. She didn't know why his brain had done this but she did know they could find out if he was still willing to continue with these sessions. It was totally up to him though. No one could make him do this. No one could do this for him. Only he could make that decision and only he could make it happen. He alone had all the power. She was apparently finished speaking then because she leaned back in her chair and sat quietly.

Mason had heard every word she'd said. He understood very clearly what she'd told him.

He let a minute pass before he finally spoke again. He told her he'd heard her and her understood her. He said he had come to dislike the chips game the more he'd played it and now he understood why. It was hard to own his emotions. He didn't want to believe he was angry and it frustrated him that people kept saying he was. The game made him face how often he actually was angry and that just frustrated him even more. He paused a moment, looked her in the eye and told her that as much as he'd grown to dislike it he was glad he'd played the game because now he knew he *really was* angry. He may not like it but he now recognized that *without doubt* anger was his go-to emotion.

Dr. Rossman smiled and told him this was real progress.

Unexpectedly, he felt the anger rising inside him again. This time instead of trying to push it down and deny it he decided to embrace it.

She saw what was happening. It wasn't often that she was unsure of how to proceed with a patient but this was one of those times. She didn't know what the root cause of his anger was. She didn't know what he had experienced that had lain dormant all these many years. But he was willing to find out and it was her job to help him get there. So she did what she did best. She pushed him, gently, at first, but then relentlessly. She questioned him as to why he was angry. She asked him repeatedly what it was he was so angry about. He answered each time that he didn't know. Still, she kept asking. He'd seemed almost irate as once again, he told her he didn't know why he was so angry. She set her face in a stern expression, looked him in the eyes, raised her voice ever so slightly and *demanded* to know.

During these past few moments as she'd been questioning him his body had begun to display all the signs of intense anxiety. Now he verbally exploded at her that he didn't know! He took a deep breath, looked around frantically and added that what he did know was that little things would often set him off. He then stood up and shouted down at her "and big things threaten to push me right over the edge!"

Dr. Rossman willed herself to sit perfectly still and show absolutely no reaction. It seemed to have a calming effect on him. It also seemed that the outburst had exhausted him as he slowly sank back down onto the couch.

Dr. Rossman sat silently watching him. His struggle was real. She could see a myriad of emotions playing themselves out across his face. After giving him a few moments to regain control she leaned forward in her chair once more before she finally posed the question she'd been wanting to ask since their first session.

"What would it look like if you were to be pushed over the edge?"

She never took her eyes off his face and there it was. Something intense flashed in his eyes.

What was going on inside him? She didn't know. The only thing she knew for sure was that this man's struggle was real.

"Mason," she said quietly.

"Mason," again, calmly, gently.

He wouldn't look at her. He was staring straight ahead.

"Mason," she said again. He still didn't respond

"Mason, I want you to know that you're safe here," she let him sit with that a moment.

"This is your safe place," she said it quietly.

"Mason, no matter what you tell me I'm not going to judge you. I'm not here to judge you. I'm only here to help you work this through. Is there anything you want to tell me, Mason?"

His breath was raspy. She could actually feel his struggle.

Suddenly his eyes darted to hers but then quickly, away again,

He didn't feel safe. He *still* didn't trust her completely. In that case there was nothing else she could do for him. She remained still and continued to wait.

Finally, he let out a heavy sigh. He raked his hands through his thick, dark hair. He leaned forward and put his face into his hands.

That's it then, she thought. He's not going to talk about it. We're done for today.

But just as she was about to end the session he lifted his head and whispered, "Something happened. *Something terrible happened.* I've never told anyone and *I'm not going to tell you.* But I will tell you this, I've got to know where my anger is coming from and deal with it because nothing like that can ever, *ever* happen again!!"

CHAPTER 24

Vonda awoke on Friday morning in the living room recliner to find daylight streaming into the room. It wasn't often that she slept the entire night in her recliner and it was definitely unusual that the morning sunlight hadn't woken her earlier. Glancing at the clock she was could hardly believe it was fast approaching nine a.m. She *absolutely never* slept that late.

Having been awake long after midnight she supposed it was to be expected. Hopefully, she'd sleep better tonight.

"Well, what's gotten into you, Lilly?" She asked her beloved feline as she realized Lilly was still snuggled up next to her and gently stroked her soft fur. "I can't believe you haven't been mewing for your breakfast by now. I guess we've both been a little out of sorts this week."

As soon as Vonda stirred in the recliner Lilly stood up, stretched and padded to the edge of the chair before gently leaping to the floor. Turning to look back up at her she then waited for Vonda. Following suit, Vonda stood, stretched, folded her throw cover neatly in half and placed it into the basket beside the chair. She then looked down at Lilly.

"Yes, I know," she spoke gently, "it's well past breakfast time. Come on girl, let's get you fed." Lilly meowed loudly as she stayed in step with Vonda all the way to her dish. "Yes, I'm sure you're hungry. You should've woken me earlier," Vonda answered while filling her dish. "That should help," she said as she walked over and pulled the blinds back from the sliders to let the fullness of the beautiful sunshine come flooding in. She immediately noticed the large cement truck backed up at the driveway of the house on Hardee Street with cement pouring out as several men spread it evenly over the drive.

"Well, isn't that exciting?" she said softly. "The new owners must be very happy today. They're another step closer to taking possession of their lovely, new house."

She wondered into the kitchen, set her mug on the base of the Keurig, inserted a new k-cup and pressed the start button. Waiting as the coffee streamed into her mug she thanked God for the gorgeous morning after such a restless night. As she'd taught herself to do in the thick of her grief she began to name everything she was thankful for. It was a wonderful way to take her focus off of her loss. She felt her spirit lifting as she wondered through the house opening the blinds and naming her many blessings. She quickly completed her morning routine of getting ready to face the day.

Returning to the kitchen she thought again about the family moving in on Hardee Street. She asked God to bless them in their new home and to help her be a good neighbor for them.

A few moments later, coffee mug in hand she slipped out the back door and settled comfortably into her rocking chair. Feeling the morning sun on her skin she continued her conversation with God, praying for her children and grandchildren as she watched the driveway being laid at the new house. The sun was already warm as it beat down on her from the cloudless sky. The slight breeze lifted strands of her hair and gently laid them down again. The tall grasses in the vacant lots danced beautifully in the wind. It was shaping up to be a wonderful day.

As she placed her mug into the dishwasher Vonda noticed it was ready to be run and started the wash cycle. Absentmindedly, she went about the chores she routinely completed each morning after her breakfast. Taking an assessment of her fridge and cupboards she prepared a grocery list before heading out to drop off her library books, pick up postage stamps at the post office, get gasoline and go grocery shopping.

A few hours later Vonda stood in the flower section of the grocery store trying to decide which of the beautiful but simple four dollar sets of flowers to purchase. She'd discovered this cheerful bargain about six months ago and had gotten into the habit of keeping fresh flowers on her dining room table. It was an inexpensive way to brighten her home and her life. She'd bought white daisy's three weeks ago and was in the mood for something colorful and bright to replace them. She was feeling light and happy, almost joyful even. There was nothing special about this day. No tangible reason for her present mood. And just like that, *in that very moment*, Vonda realized that just as suddenly as it had settled down upon her on Sunday, this most recent wave of grief had lifted. It wasn't the first time it had happened this way and she was certain it wouldn't be the last. Hopefully, there would be a longer stretch of time before it happened again. Only time would tell.

That was just the way it was with grief.

CHAPTER 25

Following through on her earlier commitment Vonda attended the second work day to continue making improvements on the building donated to Dogwood Alliance Church. This time she was part of the landscape crew whose task it was to get the grounds in order. After years of neglect there was no shortage of work to be done. The church grounds crew members were to take care of mowing the lawn, weed eating around the edges of the building and tilling the land where shrubs and flowers were to be planted.

Vonda had been thrilled to be part of the design team over the past several weeks. The team had worked together deciding which flowers were to be planted in which locations. Today she was happy to be on the planting crew. She enjoyed working side by side with the other ladies who chatted and laughed together as they planted the bulbs and starts. They excitedly envisioned how beautiful it was all going to look when the flowers took root and came to full bloom.

After completing the mornings work the group ventured inside to see how the renovations were coming along. Vonda couldn't believe the transformation that had taken place since she'd first seen the structure.

Marshall and his crew had been very busy and were hard at it again today. Seeing Vonda among the other ladies Marshall walked over to greet them. As the ladies showered compliments on him and his crew he simply stood back and smiled. He then spent a few minutes updating them on what was yet to be done. Several of the ladies thanked him for taking the time to talk with them before they all began to walk away. When Marshall asked Vonda for a moment she told the other ladies she'd catch up and waved them on.

"I'm wondering what you've got going on when we're done working today. If you're not tied up maybe we can grab a meal together. Our chats after the Thursday night ball games are great but they're not long enough to really get caught up. What do you think?"

"That's a lovely idea," Vonda answered and told him she wasn't sure how much longer her group would be working since all of the planting was done. They agreed she'd circle back through and touch base with him once she'd been dismissed. If Marshall was at a good stopping point they'd head out together. If not, they'd work out details to meet up once he was free.

Just over an hour later they were seated at El Campestre, the only Mexican place in Logan and one of Vonda's favorite eateries. She ordered her usual, the Chicken Quesadia Verde and Marshall ordered a beef Chimichanga.

The two friends sat casually chatting and munching chips and salsa as they waited for their food to arrive. Marshall was nonchalantly watching the wait staff coming and going when he noticed Carlos serving food to a table. He'd had no idea Carlos worked there. He was wondering about him working two jobs when Vonda asked how long it would be before the renovation at the church was completed. Everything else was forgotten as he answered her question.

Marshall enjoyed talking shop with Vonda. It wasn't every woman who understood or took a genuine interest in construction the way she did. As their friendship had grown Vonda had shared that her late husband was what she lovingly called a master handyman. He was excellent at home renovations and she'd worked side by side with him on many projects through the years.

As much as Marshall enjoyed talking with her, Vonda enjoyed listening when he talked about his work. Occasionally their conversations would evoke a memory of working with Stanley and she would share it with Marshall. Each of them was enjoying their new friendship and conversation flowed comfortably throughout the meal. Vonda was glad to hear things were going well with Marshall and the company as well as in his relationship with his brothers. Marshall shared that as far as he knew Mitch had been dating Lucille for almost two years. At least it had been about that since Marshall had first met her and on occasion Mitch would mention doing something with her. While it was true that he didn't actually spend time with them he could only assume the relationship to be going well. He also shared that his younger brother, Mason, had told him he was going to counseling and was quite hopeful he and Stacey would be reconciling. Their sons, Marshall's nephews, Declan and Caleb seemed to be handling their parents' separation well, which had been Mason's main concern. Marshall thanked Vonda for her continued prayers for him and his brothers. Vonda in turn updated Marshall on the most recent news from her children and other happenings in her life.

Before they parted ways Marshall told Vonda about the upcoming Davidson Construction company picnic and invited her to attend as his guest. He did explain that being the face of the company he'd be making the rounds

73

and wouldn't be able to actually spend much time with her there. Still, it would be a free meal in a beautiful setting with some interesting things to do and see. He was thinking since she was hoping to get to know more people in the area she might want to check it out. Besides, he just thought she might enjoy it. Vonda agreed it sounded like an opportunity she didn't want to miss and readily accepted his invitation.

CHAPTER 26

Just as he'd hoped would happen nothing had seemed amiss when he arrived at the Hardee Street project for his scheduled work shift the following afternoon. Probably as a result of pure exhaustion, more mental than physical, he'd fallen asleep quickly once he'd finally gotten into bed the previous night. He'd slept soundly the entire night and awoken later than usual.

He determined immediately the next morning not to allow the events of the night before to take root in his mind. Every time a memory tried to surface he pushed it aside and busied himself with something else. *Anything else.*

After he'd showered and gone over everything in his mind the night before he made the determination that he was *not* going to let this ruin his life. It was an unfortunate and undeniably traumatic event, but he'd dealt with it. Now, he was just going to have to move on, not revisiting it and *never dwelling on it.* In fact, he decided he wouldn't allow himself to think of it ever again. With that in mind the following morning he chose a multiple part documentary and watched it right up until it was time to report to the job site.

To his immense satisfaction he arrived on site to see that the cement driveway had been laid as scheduled. Everything seemed to be going on as usual. As he'd done on every previous project he had worked he immediately went straight to the newly laid driveway. He gave it the once over and commented to the eager agreement of his fellow crew members on how good the job looked. He'd then moved on to join in their discussion of the landscaping to be done around the front of the house early next week. Being as it was Friday everyone was in a jovial mood. As the afternoon went on there was talk as to what each of them had planned for the weekend. By the time he headed home that evening it felt as if the events of the day before were nothing more than a bad dream. He breathed a huge sigh of relief that life truly would go on as usual.

But nothing is ever as simple as that, is it?

By the middle of the next week he was having trouble keeping himself together. Although it was actually the perfect scenario he was finding himself growing more frustrated and confused. His confusion was a result of the fact that Victor had now missed four consecutive days of work and no one seemed to have noticed. Nothing had been mentioned about it at all. On the one hand it was the perfect solution to his problem. On the other hand, it made absolutely no sense.

As he'd done what he'd had to he had mentally prepared himself for the fact that Victor's absence from the job was going to cause a commotion. People would be talking about it. There would be a lot of speculating as to what was going on. Victor's family would most likely be notified. Everyone would be concerned. Eventually, a missing person's report would be filed and the police would be brought in.

Knowing this would be the main topic of conversation and a huge focus for everyone in the company he'd mentally prepared himself on how to react. He even had specific remarks at the ready. But instead, he'd now gone into work day after day for four days with everything going on as usual. While he knew he should be thankful it was actually causing him more stress that no one seemed to have even noticed Victor's absence. He just couldn't wrap his mind around it.

On Friday, exactly one week from the day the driveway had been laid he felt as if he could take it no longer.

Coincidentally, an opportunity presented itself when DeeDee, who literally never came to any job sites, came to the Hardee Street project. He was surprised to see her car pulling up as he was about to take his lunch break.

"Hey lady, I didn't think they ever let you out of Corporate," he called out to her with a wave as she got out of her car.

Laughingly she turned her head, waved and headed in his direction.

"Usually you'd be right about that," she answered as the wind blew her red hair into her face. She brushed it aside as she told him she'd been hearing the Hardee Street project was almost done. "I just had lunch with a friend here in Logan and I almost never get to see the finished projects so I decided to swing by and check it out on my way back."

"What a great idea," he told her as he fell in step with her.

"How about I give you the grand tour?" he asked thinking quickly that he could take advantage of this opportunity.

"Sound's great," she answered.

He'd never had any trouble talking with DeeDee. She was a breath of fresh air and just the most pleasant person to be around. There wasn't a person in the company who'd ever had an awkward moment with her. She just had a way of putting everyone at ease. Yet here he was feeling more and more stressed as he led her from room to room. Being as Victor was in the accounting department and he on the construction crew they never actually interacted. He couldn't believe how difficult it was to find a natural way to ask about Victor's absence.

Why did he even have to ask? He couldn't really answer that question. He only knew *he had to do it*. He had to find out what she'd say.

They'd gone through the house pretty quickly and were just about finished. It was now or never. Finally, not knowing what else to say he blurted out "Hey, you know when we first started this project I saw Victor getting a tour like this. I haven't seen him around lately. What gives?" As the words tumbled out he knew he'd made a huge mistake. What was she going to think? He shouldn't be the one asking about Victor. He should've just left it alone. He felt beads of perspiration standing out on his forehead and was certain she had to have noticed. Why did he have to push it? He was so caught up in his own anxiety he didn't even notice how her face lit up.

"Oh, you don't know?!" She answered excitedly. "Victor's on the most adventurous vacation in Ecuador! He was so excited when he booked it months ago. He flew out last Friday! I'm anxious to hear all about it when he gets back. He promised to take lots of pictures."

He felt himself momentarily lose his balance. He actually stumbled a bit. Reaching toward him DeeDee reacted, "Are you okay?"

He laughed awkwardly. "Sure. Sure I am, just lost my footing there for a second," he answered looking down toward his feet so she wouldn't see his shocked expression.

Victor had been leaving on vacation the very next morning?

"Wow, that's great," he added quickly. Trying not to let her see how her words had thrown him off.

"Well, listen I'd better get back to it," he said as he turned and hurried away from her.

"Yes, yes, you're right," she agreed feeling strangely. "I have to get back to it myself."

DeeDee had the distinct feeling something wasn't quite right as she headed back to her car and drove away. The problem was she had no idea what in the world could possibly be wrong.

CHAPTER 27

To Mason's own astonishment he was stepping outside his comfort zone yet again. It was almost unbelievable, especially since it was happening so soon after starting counseling. Considering what a huge step that had been it was almost inconceivable he was doing something he felt uncomfortable with again. He could actually feel the anxiety in his body as he intently watched his own feet carrying his body up the church steps and into the building.

Mason hadn't been in a church since before his parents died which now felt like a lifetime ago. Why, he hadn't even gotten married in a church. And while it was true he wasn't there for a church per se it still felt strange. During his counseling sessions he'd come to respect Dr. Rossman and he was actually growing to trust her. He was here now at her suggestion. She seemed convinced it might help him so he was willing to at least, check it out.

Having been directed to the Fellowship Hall he was now seated among strangers who were all there for the same reason.

The leaders of the group introduced themselves. A sign-in sheet was passed around and everyone was given a large booklet called Grief Share. They were then told if anyone felt this wasn't for them after this first session they were free to bow out. On the other hand, if they were willing to continue attending they'd be expected to make a thirteen week commitment. Each week would involve watching a video, filling in the blanks in the Grief Share booklet and having a group discussion. The leaders were adamant that no one had to participate in discussions if they didn't want to. However, many found it helpful.

Mason had no intention of participating. In truth he was a little embarrassed for even being there. His parents had died twenty five years earlier. Surely the time for going to a grief share program had come and gone. But Dr. Rossman told him it wasn't unusual for people to attend many years after the actual death that had impacted their life. She felt strongly this program would explain the surprising ways in which unresolved grief can spill out. She seemed fairly certain Mason would find something helpful and had strongly encouraged him to give it a chance.

So here he was.

At the end of the first session people were given the opportunity to share with the group what had brought them to the meeting. True to their word the leaders pressured no one to participate. Mason sat quietly listening to those who chose to share. Most of the losses were recent, as in within the past one to three years. Several had lost a parent, others their spouse. A few had lost a child and a few their sibling. One poor woman had lost her entire family in a tragic house fire five years ago and by her own assessment she'd come a long way. She was here because she was still struggling. To Mason, that seemed understandable after such a great loss. As he sat listening to their stories he felt great compassion for these people. Some of the situations they shared tugged at his heart strings. He still wasn't sure he belonged there but he didn't see the harm in attending. If nothing else perhaps it would give him a greater appreciation for those he was still blessed to have in his life. Besides, he was on a self-improvement journey in his counseling and this seemed to go hand in hand with that.

Because it was being offered by the church Mason had been concerned it might be overly religious. He was pleased that hadn't been accurate. It did touch on God and used scripture verses to make certain points but not excessively. It didn't come across as preachy or condemning either.

Mason remembered his parents taking them to church when he was little. He liked the classes and always had fun showing them what he'd colored or made during Sunday school. He could still remember many of the Bible stories, though not in great detail. Mason had always found it strange that on rare occasions some of the fun little songs they'd sang would, even now, rattle around inside his head. He guessed that was because he was an avid music lover.

When their parents died, Marshall came to live with his younger brothers and church was simply never mentioned again. Marshall was a man by then and hadn't been around much except for when he'd show up at the boys sporting events. Of course, he was always there on Holiday's and occasionally he'd come over for dinner. He was never at church though. Mason just assumed that was why they'd never gone to church once he became their guardian. They'd never talked about it really. There were lots of things the three brothers had never talked about.

Mason did remember feeling as if his life was out of control at that point. And it truly was. There's no control over when your parents die. And if it happens when you're young you have no control over who you stay with or what you do with your time or what you plan for your future after that.

Mason hadn't cared that he didn't get to go back to church. He was what – just fourteen at that time? He'd realized by then that he didn't really fit in with the other kids anyway. As they'd approached their teen years, groups had begun to form and for whatever reason he hadn't fallen into a particular group. Now that he was thinking about this he began to remember that he'd actually been arguing with his parents frequently about going to church. He'd wanted the freedom to choose how much time to spend with church friends and how much time to spend with friends from the neighborhood and from school. For whatever reason, his parents were a bit overly protective. He did remember that he and Mitch had been in agreement on that point. Mason was surprised he was thinking about all of this right now. He hadn't thought about any of it in years. He didn't see how it would help with what he was currently dealing with in his life but he had to admit it was interesting to think about.

Certainly losing his parents at that young age had to have had a huge impact on the rest of his life. By the end of the evening Mason felt comfortable being part of the grief share group. Knowing he wouldn't be pressured to participate in the discussions was helpful. All things considered, Mason decided he was willing to commit to the thirteen week program. He could only hope to learn something helpful in the process.

On the drive back to his apartment he was thankful he and his brothers weren't so involved in each other's lives that they divulged everything to each other. He was under no obligation to tell them about this. He wasn't thankful to be living apart from Stacey and the boys but at least that offered him the ability to do this alone. He had no intention of telling anyone he was attending a Grief Share program. At least, not until he saw how it all played out.

CHAPTER 28

Vonda had been looking forward to today ever since Marshall had invited her to attend the Davidson Construction Company's office picnic. The weather was perfect and it promised to be a beautiful day.

She was proud of herself for, once again, stepping out of her comfort zone. She hardly knew anyone from the company and Marshall was going to be tied up. Knowing she'd be on her own she was choosing to go anyway.

She chose a lovely flowered sundress and sandals for the occasion. Feeling festive she pulled a bunch of her hair up into a messy bun leaving the rest to hang loosely down across her shoulders. She felt pretty and had enjoyed dressing up a little bit. Smiling as she set the alarm code before heading out the front door Vonda had absolutely no idea how lovely she looked.

The Davidson Construction Company had rented out the old Fair Grounds for the day. After parking her car Vonda made her way across the field toward the obvious location of the festivities. From the look of things they'd gone all out for the occasion.

As Vonda leisurely strolled through she passed bouncy houses, games, pony rides, petting areas and face painting stations for the children. She also saw corn hole, horse shoe and dart throwing competitions for the adults. There was a hay maze set up as well. Signs pointed the way to the concession areas where a catering company provided a variety of snack foods and drinks along with a choice of lunches.

Vonda had no idea how large Marshall's company was but it seemed to her that there was a very good turnout. She felt happy as she walked along observing the various activities. So many people were there with their families and everyone looked to be having a wonderful time.

Since Vonda loved animals she spent quite a while petting the goats and deer and interacting with the children and parents who were doing the same. She ran into Mason who was there with his sons, Declan and Caleb. She and Mason chatted while the boys followed a couple of goats around. After they'd parted ways she enjoyed standing by to watch the children take pony rides. She was having a great time and was glad she'd decided to come.

Feeling a bit hungry Vonda went over to the concession area. It wasn't easy to decide between the featured lunches but she finally settled on the cheeseburger platter. Vonda loved a good grilled burger and didn't often get one since she didn't grill herself.

She took the first vacant seat she found which happened to be beside a couple who were around her own age. Vonda introduced herself and sat down next to the woman. It wasn't long before they were all engaged in an enjoyable conversation. The husband finished eating ahead of the women and told his wife he wanted to get in on the corn-hole competition. She was enjoying her chat with Vonda and told him he could go ahead and she'd catch up with him later.

The two ladies sat talking together for quite some time after they'd finished their meal. Being around the same age they had no trouble finding things in common to chat about. Eventually, they wondered off together and took the long way over to where they found the woman's husband deep in competition.

Vonda wondered around alone watching the various competitions. Marshall caught her by surprise when he came up beside her and told her he'd be competing in the dart throwing soon. A short time later they met up with Manny and Saul who were his dart throwing partners. By the time the official competition was to start both the other men's wives and children had arrived. Introductions were made all around and Vonda had a wonderful time sitting with those two families while they cheered for their team.

Vonda was impressed with how much the company was doing for their employees and families. To her mind the entire picnic would've been enough but throughout the entire day there had been random drawings for gifts ranging from small appliances all the way up to flat screen TV's and Laptop Computers. There were smiles all around and the general atmosphere was positive and fun. She could see that the morale of the company was high.

The picnic was slated to end with a round of fireworks just after dark. Around dusk people started to congregate in the field where the fireworks show was to take place. Marshall took the microphone and thanked everyone for coming. He gave a warmhearted speech in which he talked about the history of the company, the exciting expansion they'd experienced this year and their hopes and plans for the future. He thanked each employee emphasizing the importance of each person and thanking them for their team work which he said was what it took to make a company such as this one successful. There was a hearty round of applause as he took a seat near

Vonda. The fireworks display, though not elaborate, seemed like the perfect way to end the day.

Just before the finale Marshall apologetically told Vonda he was going to have to desert her as he needed to help with all the clean up now that the day was ending. She said she'd been surprised to have had seen him at all, told him what an enjoyable day she'd had and thanked him again for inviting her.

CHAPTER 29

He couldn't believe what he was hearing. He had no idea who this woman was but he *definitely knew* what she was referring to.

He'd simply been eating his lunch at the company picnic. Minding his own business when the conversation of the two women seated directly behind him caught his attention. The women were telling each other they occasionally had trouble sleeping when this woman started describing her most recent night of insomnia. She was awake very late one night when she began looking out her window. It was fairly bright since the moon was almost full. After just a few minutes she'd noticed some strange repetitive lighting several lots away from her house that she simply couldn't explain. As she continued describing what she'd seen he knew *exactly what it was*. It was the moonlight reflecting on his shovel *as he buried Victor's body*! He remembered how thankful he'd been that the moon was bright enough that he could see what he was doing. But now, he was thinking that might not have been so good for him. He'd felt his body tensing up as he'd sat listening. When he first realized what she was describing his heart had begun beating faster. Now there was a small catch in his throat - he actually struggled to get his breath. He was beginning to feel clammy and his hands were sweating.

He hadn't thought about that night since it had happened. Every time his mind tried to return there he'd pushed the thoughts away, turned on music or busied himself with one task or another. He didn't want to think about it *now either* but her words had immediately put him back there. It was actually as though he was there in the darkness this very moment watching as he shoveled the dirt onto Victor's still form. He couldn't stay there, mentally. *He just couldn't!* He had to get hold of himself before someone looked at him a little too closely and realized something was wrong. He had to calm his body down and the only way to do that was to steer his thoughts away from that night.

Even as he tried changing focus he turned his thoughts and his ears back to the woman speaking. He needed to know what else she'd seen. He began to feel a bit relieved when his listening revealed that, in fact, she had absolutely no idea *what she'd actually seen*. At the time it had made her curious enough to open the sliders and step outside onto to her back patio. That was when she'd heard the strange clunking sounds. As he listened to her description he realized that would've been him shoveling. She went on to say it didn't last much longer and when the strange sounds ended the strange light went away as well. After waiting in silence a few more moments she'd gone back into her house and shut the sliders. He breathed a sigh of relief as he realized she must've come outside *just before* he'd finished the job. It didn't give her much to go on now. And that was *very good* for him.

"The next day everything was back to normal in the neighborhood, so whatever it was must've been harmless," he heard her conclude to his great relief.

His body was still reacting anxiously, which would never do. If anyone noticed they'd want to know what was wrong. Since obviously, *something must be wrong*. He concentrated on breathing normally and willed himself to remain calm and appear uninterested, all the while straining to listen as she continued talking. What was that she was saying now? Something about noticing a vehicle driving by with no lights? *Oh, good god*! That had been him leaving the area after he'd finished!

Someone slapped him on the shoulder and he just about jumped out of his skin. He'd been so intent on the conversation behind him he hadn't seen or heard his coworkers approaching. He turned to find Saul and his entire family gathering around him. They were all laughing and talking about what a great day it was for the company picnic. Looking at his almost empty plate Saul's wife began guessing whether he'd had the BBQ chicken dinner or the cheeseburger platter. He laughed loudly as he tried to appear normal. When Saul's son started raving about the BBQ Chicken he made sure to agree and went into complimenting the catering service the company had chosen. They all got into a good natured argument over which meal had been the best. Saul said something about having listened to a lot of talk throughout the day and the general consensus seemed to be in favor of the food this year. He wanted to be sure to relay that information to Marshall, as they should use the same caterer for next year's picnic.

He was trying to participate in the conversation but it was difficult to pull his mind away from that woman. He desperately needed to know what else she'd seen on that fatal night.

Five more minutes passed before he could comfortably beg his way out of accompanying the group and they went on their way. A quick glance assured him the two women were still seated behind him. They were talking about something entirely different now, though. That was frustrating. He wanted to hear what else she had to say about that night. But he didn't even know her. There was simply no way he could incorporate himself into their conversation. Even if he could how could he justify asking about what he'd overheard? Who was she, anyway? He knew practically everyone at the company. He'd never seen her before and yet she was here at the Davidson Construction Company picnic.

He had no idea how to go about it he was going to have to find out who she was. He couldn't have her going around telling people what she'd seen and heard, could he? She didn't know what any of it meant but he certainly knew! Was it possible for anyone else to put it together? Could he take that chance? If not, what could he possibly do about it?

He cursed his rotten luck for the timing of being interrupted as he'd been listening. Now he may never know what else she'd witnessed. On second thought, he decided luck was still on his side. Whatever she'd witnessed she was still puzzling over herself. So she obviously hadn't been able to put it together as anything meaningful.

Reluctantly, he went back to that night in his mind and tried to analyze what exactly she could know that would be a threat to him. The last thing he'd heard her say was that she'd noticed a truck driving with no headlights on. He'd looked around before heading out that night. He'd seen no sign of anyone being awake before he pulled onto the road. Which house did she live in, anyway? Then he remembered the house with the light on. Yes, he'd noticed it at the time. He'd quickly dismissed it after he assumed the home owner simply left a lamp on as a night light. That *had to be* her house. And again, it was just his rotten luck that she was awake on that particular night at that particular time to notice his movements.

Those were the thoughts that gnawed at him for the rest of the day. He didn't enjoy the rest of the company picnic at all. *How could he?* He was obsessed with what he'd heard and worried about who this woman was and who else she would talk to about her restless night.

In one moment he'd tell himself none of it mattered. After all, no one even realized Victor was missing! They weren't even looking for him - let alone his body. *None* of what she'd seen or heard could be connected to him, especially since someone *had yet* to realize Victor was missing! In the next moment, he'd be overcome with anxiety that somehow this woman was going to be his undoing.

He set his mind to enjoying the rest of the day but it was a struggle. In the end he left earlier than he normally would've and felt compelled to drive past the Hardee Street house. Even though he'd worked on the new houses currently being built right next door many times since that fateful night. He'd even waved at the new owners on several occasions. They were a friendly, older couple. Logically, he already knew nothing was amiss but he had to drive by just to assure himself all was well. And that, still, no one was the wiser. As he drove by he couldn't help but think of poor Victor, dead under that driveway.

He looked across the vacant lots toward the woman's house. He could actually envision her opening the door and standing outside just as he'd heard her say she'd done that night. She'd been out there looking and listening. Oh, why did she have to be restless that night? And what was he going to do about it?

CHAPTER 30

It surprised Mason how quickly and easily he'd gotten comfortable with the other members of the Grief Share group. In the beginning session he'd wondered if he belonged there and exactly how he fit in as they worked their way through certain things being normal in the grieving process. Things like being unable to focus, being forgetful, feeling numb, and feeling like you're just going through the motions in daily life. Most of those symptoms happen immediately following the loss of a loved one.

Mason had no memory of dealing with any of that but considering that his parents had died twenty five years before he attended Grief Share he supposed it made sense. One session dealt with avoiding places that remind you of your loved one and not wanting to change their bedroom or part with their personal items. Again, having only been fourteen at the time his folks died none of that applied to him.

It wasn't until the session exploring the difficulty others may have understanding you and how grief affects your other relationships, that Mason was able to identify things in his own life which could've been an impact of grief.

In between the sessions Mason found himself remembering some of the thoughts and emotions he'd experienced so long ago.

The sixth session was the first one Mason could personally relate to. It dealt exclusively with questioning the fairness of losing someone so important in your life, perhaps even questioning God. Mason didn't remember having those specific thoughts. He did remember an overall feeling of the unfairness of life hovering over him during the first couple of years after his parents died. To have your parents die together at such an early point in your life just didn't seem fair at all. It still didn't seem fair as he looked at it now, from the viewpoint of a grown man. He found himself asking God why it had to happen. Yes, it was a terrible accident. Just an unfortunate life situation but if God was the loving God his childhood church had taught about how and why would He do this to Mason, Mitch and Marshall? As Mason struggled through these challenging thoughts he began to realize it wasn't the first time.

It was becoming clear to him that since the three brothers had just gone on in life adjusting to their new situation without talking about the loss of their parents, he'd struggled through those things alone. Grief Share was reawakening those memories. Exploring and discussing these issues in the present time Mason now felt free to admit he'd placed blame and felt angry with God. The leadership of the Grief Share group encouraged talking with God very honestly about these things. After all, they pointed out, if He really is God, He's strong enough to deal with our true emotions, thoughts and resentments, even the ones toward Him. If He truly loves humanity He'll love us despite those things.

Dr. Rossman's prediction that this group would be helpful for Mason was proving true. One of the group members whom Mason could really relate to was Nelson. Nelson's wife had recently passed away after a long, tough fight with a brain tumor. She'd gone from being a vibrant, active woman to being wheelchair bound and losing all ability to reason. Nelson was her main caregiver. When she died Nelson began attending this Grief Share session.

Interestingly enough, during the weekly fill-in-the-blank and discussion session Nelson had become more and more verbal about his father's death over twenty years ago. Nelson was surprised to realize he'd been hanging onto anger toward his father all those years. He'd been especially close to his father and his dad had verbally promised Nelson he'd always be there for him. Of course, intellectually Nelson knew it wasn't his dad's choice to die suddenly, at a young age, leaving his young son behind. Emotionally, his dad's death had been devastating. It felt like a broken promise and the epitome of abandonment.

To make matters worse his dad died of a massive heart attack on Nelson's eighth birthday in the middle of his birthday party. His mother made a cake and gave him gifts each year after that but Nelson never agreed to a birthday party again and never truly celebrated his birthday in his spirit.

It was true that Nelson's wife had recently died and he was definitely grieving for her. Still, Mason found it interesting that the program seemed to be awakening in Nelson many issues that were a direct result of his father's death during his childhood. Mason was beginning to wonder what impact of his own parents' deaths during his childhood may've had on him.

CHAPTER 31

It had now been three days since the company picnic. He'd been unable to think clearly for even one of them. He'd been going over and over what he'd heard that woman saying and what he hadn't heard but wished he had. His mind was constantly tormenting him. What did she know that she didn't even realize she knew? Who was she? His mind was running rampart with conflicting thoughts. He was tempted to do something about her but kept deciding it was best to do nothing. In the end, the only real reason he hadn't done something was that without knowing who she was he had no idea where to start.

Then suddenly and unexpectedly fate intervened.

Marshall decided to do a big push among his employees to try to increase participation on the Old Timer's baseball team. In hopes of enticing new players to join in he'd made an announcement at work on Monday inviting them out to play on Thursday but this time he added a twist.

Being as many of his crews were under age for the team he issued a challenge for those younger to form a team and prove they could get the best of the Old Timers. A game would ensue between the two age groups as long as enough players came out. It was his hope that a few more of his older employees would show up. He was certain once they'd played they'd want to join the team. He was convinced participating in the sport would be good for their overall health. Marshall had made the announcement each day all week long. It was now Thursday and Marshall had spent the bulk of the day compelling his workers to come out and participate.

His evening plans had fallen through at the last minute. Being at loose ends and now having no reason not to go to the ball field, he'd gone. The game was in the third inning when he noticed a woman seated in the stands cheering loudly. He quickly realized it was *her*. The *same woman* he'd overheard at the company picnic.

From that moment on he was obsessed with her. He kept watching her out of the corner of his eye. It wasn't long before he noticed that although she was cheering for most of the players she cheered just a bit louder for Marshall. Sometimes Marshall would actually turn toward her and pump his arms in a winners fashion or make some other gesture and she'd laugh. It was obvious they not only knew each other, they were friends. Was that why she'd been at the company picnic? Thinking back over the day he was sure he hadn't seen Marshall anywhere near her, so it still didn't make sense.

Once the game ended he purposefully hung around the ball field just to see what she did. She chatted with several groups of spectators in the stands, even walking toward their vehicles with a few of them only to return to the field each time. He'd gone to his vehicle and was seated in the driver's seat.

Unnoticed, he sat watching.

When most everyone else was gone she tagged along chatting with Marshall while he gathered up the equipment and put everything away. It looked like Marshall was offering her a ride. She refused, stepped back and waved and started off on foot. Realizing she'd walked to the game he impulsively put the car in drive and quickly drove toward her house. He decided to park on the vacant dirt road behind her house where all the wooded lots were still waiting to be purchased and built on. He then sneaked through the woods. Finding a spot where he could clearly see her back patio he simply stopped and waited.

Fortunately, he'd worn his black jeans and t-shirt to the ball field. Before getting out of his car he'd put on the black hoodie he always kept there. He was certain he'd gone unnoticed since darkness was falling quickly and he'd seen absolutely no one out and about.

Soon he saw the light go on in her living area. He had a pretty clear view of the dinning and kitchen area through the sliders as she hadn't drawn the blinds yet. Every now and then she'd pass by the sliders and go into the kitchen and move around a bit. There was a large white cat following her every move. At one point they both stood in front of the sliders lazily looking out over the back yard. He felt strange watching her this way but he also felt strongly compelled to do so.

Being there gave him a clear picture of what had happened the night he buried Victor's body. He could see exactly where she would've stood on her patio looking over to the right, in the South East direction, toward the Hardee Street house. While the entire other direction from her back patio was all wooded there were only open fields between her house and the house where Victor was now buried. If he hadn't been almost done when she stepped out she may've actually been able to see him. He had to thank his lucky stars that hadn't happened.

The area where he was standing was made up of wooded plots that butted up to the back of her property. It, too, was waiting to be purchased and built on. At the end of the woods and on to the next lot that joined her property is where the land became fields. The field area was made up of five vacant lots waiting to be sold for new housing development. It was all part of the Hardee Street Project. He'd be building homes in this area for the rest of this year and well into next, most likely.

The longer he leaned there against that tree in the darkness watching her move around inside her house the more comfortable he grew. He picked up some useful information just by watching. Her house was protected by a security alarm system. The entire back side of the house was well lit by her patio lights which were bright and lit up the entire area. If he were to need to get to her he'd have to do it from the front of the house.

When he left he drove around to the front of her house, parked his car a few doors down and studied that area. There was lighting in the front but with her entry being recessed her front door wasn't visible to her side neighbors. A vacant lot stood across the street so there were no neighbors directly across from the front of the house who might see something. She had large, tall hedges growing on either side of her front entry. He could see how one could easily stay hidden behind those until she arrived home or came out the front door. All they'd have to do then would be to come in from behind cover her mouth with something to make her pass out and drag her behind the tall hedges. All of that could be accomplished in a matter of minutes. Tall shrubs stood all along the front area of the house. The side yard was in darkness and there was only one very short distance in the lighted area between the house and the back shed which backed up to the woods. From there she could easily be carried to a waiting vehicle.

Even as he thought this all out he wasn't thinking of actually taking her. *Of course not.*

CHAPTER 32

Mason's ears perked up during the Grief Share discussion when Nelson began to talk about having struggled with anger his whole life but never, until now, knowing why. He seemed to be experiencing great relief and freedom now that he was making the connection.

Nelson shared what it was like being able to look back at himself at 8 years old. He could now see and totally understand how he, as a child, could be angry at his father not only for ruining his birthday party, but for dying and leaving the family. Although Nelson had remained faithful to his spiritual beliefs throughout his entire life he now understood why he'd had such a spiritual struggle.

He talked quite openly about how freeing it was to realize and admit he'd been angry at God all these years for letting his dad die. Nelson was having a renewed relationship with God now.

As Mason witnessed this unfolding in Nelson's life it gave him the ability to open his own eyes and heart. He began to examine his own feelings in regard to the death of his parents. Mason quickly discovered that the more he allowed himself to think about his parents' deaths the more he was opening memories of his parents' lives.

He hadn't given it much thought before attending Grief Share but he never actually thought about them. He had literally shut them completely out of his life when they died. In trying to analyze this he wondered how much of it was due to the fact that once Marshall became legal guardian over his brothers there was simply no talk about their parents. He didn't blame Marshall. Marshall was only twenty five years old and in the midst of a successful career as he pursued running his own company. It was a lot for a young man to handle.

Mason was now able to identify the introverted personalities of both Marshall and Mitch. Their mother was an introvert, too. Mason on the other hand, was extroverted, like their father. Being introverts neither of his brothers were inclined to talk things out unless provoked. It was only natural that the terrible tragedy that had cost them their parents had gotten locked away.

Mason being the youngest of the brothers hadn't known how to let his older brothers know what he needed. He hadn't even recognized his need to verbalize his memories, his loss and the emotions that went along with it all. So he said nothing and time simply passed. Mason could see now that he'd actually pushed his feelings, memories and emotions deep down in an attempt to survive.

Now, through his counseling sessions with Dr. Rossman and the information he was gaining at Grief Share Mason could see that hadn't been good for him. Oh, he'd survived but in a damaged way.

It was no wonder he often felt frustrated and angry. He still couldn't specifically pinpoint the anger but it was beginning to make more sense. Was it possible for frustration to actually become anger? He didn't know, but for the first time in his life he was open to finding out.

Listening to Nelson talking about the day his dad died had been heart wrenching for Mason. He could just imagine that eight year old boy watching his dad die of a sudden massive heart attack during his birthday party.

Driving home after that session Mason allowed his own mind to travel back to the day of his parents' death. For the first time in all those years he became a fourteen year old boy trying to absorb such terrible news. These two people he'd depended on since day one were suddenly not to be depended on ever again. They were gone and they *were never coming back!*

It was with great surprise that Mason found himself reaching up to wipe a tear from his face. He couldn't believe it. He was actually grieving the loss of his parents twenty five years after their death.

As the evening wore on he found himself remembering their mother's sweet smile, the way she'd laugh quickly and loudly and her loving hugs every morning before he went out the door for school. He then remembered that once he'd reached Jr. High she'd had to push him to get a quick hug. It was at that age he began trying to avoid letting her hug him. Her pursuit of a hug had become a morning ritual for the two of them. On those occasions when she succeeded her delighted laughter would follow him as he went out the door to catch the school bus. He never would have admitted it to her then, but he now remembered that most times he smiled to himself once he was on the bus. At some point it had gone from being an avoidance of her affection to just a fun game they were playing. He found himself wishing he could tell her that now.

With the influx of memories of his mother it was only natural for memories of his dad to resurface. The next morning he found himself

94

suddenly standing with his dad on the boat ramp as they anticipated their early morning fishing trip. In this memory they'd double checked their equipment before stepping down into the canoe and shoving off. The sun was just starting it's ascent over the horizon. The air was cool and thick as they dipped their oars into the muddy water and guided the canoe to their favorite fishing spot.

He and dad were the only two early birds in the family and this had been their thing. Early morning fishing trips on the creek that ran through the back of their home property and joined the river up-stream. Mason hadn't been in a canoe or fishing since his father's death.

What a loss.

What an incredible loss.

CHAPTER 33

He reached into the Krispie Kreme box and pulled out an apple fritter. DeeDee could always be counted on to have special treats, like fritters, at unscheduled meetings. She knew unexpected meetings put people in foul moods and good food was the way to turn those frowns into smiles. She was one smart lady. He always tried to arrive early at these meetings to get first pick of whatever delicacy she provided.

Sure enough there were lots of scowls on the faces filing into the room. The donuts seemed to be helping with the overall mood though.

He asked a few people nearest him if they had any idea what was going on. No one seemed to know anything except that the companywide email had gone out at two o'clock stating there was a mandatory meeting at four thirty at Corporate, so here they were.

He couldn't remember the last time they'd all been called in at once. It had him wondering what was going on - he and everyone else in the building. There wasn't enough seating even though they were in the largest conference room at Corporate. A good number of folks were standing along the walls. Everyone was hoping this wouldn't take long.

Marshall was trying to get everyone's attention but his voice was drowning out in the loud chatter of the room. Finally, he clapped his hands together and fired off a shrill whistle to get everyone's attention.

The room went silent immediately.

"Thank you for coming in on such short notice," Marshall said to the now attentive room.

Like we had a choice was the thought of more than one annoyed employee in the room.

"I know this is inconvenient and interferes with your busy schedules but I'm sure you'll realize the importance once we've explained. Something vital has come to our attention and we need your help. I'm going to ask that you give your undivided attention to this meeting and stay afterward if you've got any information at all, even if it doesn't seem important. Please bring it forward so the authorities can decide if it's pertinent."

By this point everyone was wondering what he was talking about. A serious quiet had settled over the room as Marshall turned toward the door of the conference room, stretched out his hand and said, "Please come in officers. We're ready for you."

Two uniformed police officers entered the room followed by a man in a dark grey business suit, black shirt and light grey necktie. That man walked straight to the front of the room flanked by the officers. The men in uniform shook Marshall's hand and quietly thanked him. The man in the suit did the same and then all of them turned to face the room with the suited man taking center stage.

"Good afternoon, everyone, my name is Andrew Wood and I'm the Lead Detective for the Stokesbury SC Police Department. I have with me two of our department's finest officers who will be gathering information from you in just a few minutes."

Everyone turned to look at each other in curiosity and surprise.

"I'm sorry to alarm you, but after speaking with Mr. Davidson at some length earlier today we've collectively decided this is the best way to get the most information in the least amount of time. What we're dealing with is a missing person and unfortunately, in these cases it's possible some type of foul play, criminal behavior, if you will, may also be involved."

He felt himself growing warm as realization dawned on him.

This was it.

It was happening.

He concentrated on keeping his breathing slow and steady. He told himself there was nothing to worry about. All he had to do was sit calmly and listen like everyone else. Draw no attention and leave as soon as the meeting was dismissed.

The detective went on, "After we've explained the situation I ask that those of you who have any information pertaining to the missing person, stay behind and fill us in. As your CEO has already stated we're interested in *any information at all*. Even if it doesn't seem like much to you we ask that you stay and relay it. This will accelerate the investigation process. The sooner we find this man the better it'll be for everyone. Finally, if anyone in this room has heard from Victor Tonnae over the past ten days please raise your hand or come forward at this point." He and his two officers stood looking intently around the room.

No one moved except to cast sideways glances at each other to see if anyone was responding. A few people who knew and worked closely with

Victor began to react to the fact that he was apparently missing. After about thirty seconds Lead Detective Wood asked more pointedly.

"Has anyone in this room had any form of contact with Victor Tonnae within the last ten days?"

Still no response.

"Okay, we're going to have to backtrack. It's my understanding that this is the date of the last day Victor was at work," he held up a black board with a date written on it. "At this time I'll ask that all those who saw, spoke to or communicated in any way with Victor Tonnae on this date remain in the room after we dismiss the meeting. We need to speak with everyone who interacted with Victor on his last scheduled work day. Anyone else with any information about Victor, please stay in this room, as well. The rest of you please write down the names and phone numbers on this board or take a picture on your phones. At any point in the future, please call me or one of these two officers if anything comes to mind that may help us locate Victor Tonnae."

At that point the meeting was turned back over to Marshall who briefly explained that Victor had left work that Thursday and to everyone's understanding he was to fly out for his vacation the next morning. Unfortunately, his vehicle had recently been located and brought to the attention of the police. The police had contacted Victor's family who informed the police of his vacation plans and that he was to visit them after his trip. Thus far, no one had heard from him.

Further investigation revealed that Victor never made it onto the flight he was to take the next day. The family told Detective Wood where Victor was employed. At that point the Detective contacted the company and was put in touch with Marshall.

Marshall talked about Victor fondly for a few moments touching on what an invaluable part of Davidson Construction Victor had become. He added that this was a very concerning situation. DeeDee was standing near the door sniffling quietly and wiping her tears with a tissue. Several other people were reacting, as well. Overall, there was a general spirit of unrest throughout the room. Marshall thanked everyone for coming, reminded those who'd been instructed to remain behind to stay. He then dismissed the meeting.

Getting up from his place at the table he walked solemnly past those who were staying behind. So, it's finally happening. He thought as he purposefully avoided a group of his colleagues standing in the hallway talking about the meeting. He forced himself to remain calm and unnoticed as he left the building. As he drove away he breathed in and let out a deep sigh in an attempt to release the tension from his body.

So Victor's car had been discovered. Well, he'd known it would happen.

Now all he had to do was stay out of the fray while the police investigated. Victor hadn't told anyone of his suspicions. He's said that himself the night he died. He reminded himself he was in the clear. All he had to do was remember that. He could count on that. Remain silent and stay out of the picture. Easy-peasy. There was nothing to tie Victor to him any more than to any other person in the company. If all went as planned, and it would, eventually the case would go cold and be forgotten. Nothing in his daily life was going to change.

CHAPTER 34

He'd started out so well, remaining calm. Repeating over and over everything he'd told himself in the meeting that revealed Victor as a missing person.

He did great until he remembered the *one person* who could ruin everything. He still didn't know for sure what she had seen when she noticed his truck leaving with the lights off that night. He was interrupted when overhearing her and never heard the rest of her tale of woe from that sleepless night.

He behaved normally as he interacted with people over the next few hours. But his mind wouldn't stop churning and he began obsessing over it. He finally convinced himself he had to silence her. He couldn't risk her talking about what she'd seen and heard.

She could be his undoing.

Acting fast he'd gotten everything he needed to deal with the situation. Truthfully, he had been thinking this through ever since the company picnic. He didn't *want* to do anything to her, the fact that it had come to that was her own fault. If she hadn't been talking about it he'd never have known. He'd never have had to worry about someone putting things together. But she did talk, he did hear and now he had to deal with it. It was just the way it was.

He had no idea what her schedule was or whether she'd be at home at this time or not. He was just going to have to wing it. By the time he arrived it was getting dark. He drove his car, instead of his truck, since he'd never taken the car when he was working on the Hardee Street projects. If it were seen in that neighborhood no one would tie it to the company.

He turned the lights off when he made the turn onto the same road he'd parked on before. He drifted off the road and into the wooded area just enough for the car to go unnoticed under cover of darkness. Again, he had donned all black. He put on the black hoodie and made his way through the woods to the back of her house. It only took a few moments to ascertain she wasn't at home. Talk about blind luck! He crept to the front of the house and took his position behind the tall shrub flanking her recessed front entryway. Once there he simply waited.

Hidden in the dark he continued to wrestle with himself as to whether or not he *had* to do this. Despite how uncomfortable it made him, he kept arriving at the same conclusion. He had to do it. He couldn't risk having her reveal what she'd witnessed, having it put together and Victor's body being found. Hiding there in the dark he went over his plan repeatedly. She *had to be silenced* before it was too late. Still, he didn't feel good about doing this.

She seemed like a nice woman. She was Marshall's friend, even. He wished there were another way. Maybe he *was* being hasty. Maybe he should think this through a bit more. These were his thoughts right up to the moment that a car approached the house. He was pressed up against the wall behind him still thinking of aborting the mission when the car turned in the driveway.

She was home.

Vonda didn't enjoy coming home after dark. It had taken a long time, over a year in fact, after she lost Stanley before she'd been willing to stay out late in the evenings since it meant returning to the house after dark. But eventually she'd gotten braver. Reminding herself that nothing scary had ever happened, she lived in a safe neighborhood and she didn't want to restrict herself by living in fear.

The first time she stayed out past dark it was to attend a Christmas concert. She was trying to get into the spirit of the season. That wasn't easy since it was her first year without Stanley. A local church was having an evening service of Christmas music. She loved Christmas music and *really wanted* to be there. Despite her overwhelming sense of fear she made herself go. She was so proud of herself when she was safely home and back in her house at the end of the evening.

It wasn't long after that victory that she'd decided to try the Wednesday night Bible Study at her church. Practice makes perfect and she'd now gotten pretty comfortable going each week. She sometimes still felt a little uneasy coming home after dark.

It always helped when she reminded herself that she lived in a very safe area. God was with her and would protect her. She told herself those things again now as she put her purse across her shoulder and gathered her Bible from the front seat of the car. She had some extra papers from the lesson tonight and was struggling to carry everything as she approached the front door. She stepped into the recessed entry area at the front of her house, put the key into the key hole and turned the doorknob. Making sure she hadn't dropped anything she paused and looked down. Suddenly, a strong arm came around her. She was grabbed by one hand while the other arm stretched around her and held both of her arms tightly against her body. Instinctively, she struggled. Fighting against them, trying to get away from whoever this was. *What's happening?* Her mind screamed as a strong smelling cloth covered her mouth and nose. "Oh, no! *NO!*" her mind screamed as she tried to twist free. She continued struggling but he was just too strong and the chloroform was working its way into her system. It wasn't long before she knew it was no use. She was going down.

As she went limp in his arms everything she'd been holding fell at their feet. He hadn't counted on that. He had envisioned a smooth capture. Stay calm. He thought to himself. No one can see this area. He leaned down and hurriedly grabbed up the items she'd dropped. She's so small and light. He thought as he pressed her limp body to the front of himself and crept back behind the bush. Quickly he made his way behind the hedges, along the house to the corner where he would turn to be at the side yard. Covered in darkness, and staying close to the house he made it to the back corner. He was now facing the only lighted area he would have to pass through. He took a deep breath and calmed himself. He turned her body toward him and hoisted her up over his shoulder still clutching the miscellaneous items she'd dropped in his free hand. He looked around intently taking in the entire neighborhood. He saw no movement anywhere. No one was around. He heard no voices or vehicles. Feeling safe he made the dash across the thirty five foot area that fell within the realm of her back porch lights. Soon he was through the woods. Arriving at his car he quietly laid her across the back seat and drove quickly away.

CHAPTER 35

He drove her to the secluded location that had come to mind as soon as he'd considered that things may come to this. There were a few furnishings still there. He took her inside and laid her down on the old couch. He folded a black bandana and tied it over her eyes making sure she couldn't see him if she happened to come to.

His heart was racing. He couldn't believe what he was doing. He wasn't feeling confidant with this at all. He turned her over, pulled her hands together and used the thick strip tie to bind them together at the wrists. He turned her back around.

Remembering the things she'd dropped and trying to be thorough he forgot about gagging her and went to his car to gather them up. Carrying them inside he sat down and looked to see what he was holding.

What's this? He asked himself as he looked down at the book in his hand. A Bible? She'd been carrying *a Bible* when he took her? Having a Bible in his hands at that moment didn't feel right at all. He quickly shoved the loose papers inside it and laid it on the floor next to her. There that was better.

She looks so small, he thought as he stood looking down at her. What was he doing? What had he been thinking to take her and bring her here? Oh, dear God, what had he gotten himself into now?

"No, don't do that," he said aloud. "You have a plan. You know what you have to do. Just stick to the plan and everything will be alright." But even as he talked himself through it a sour taste was rising up in his throat. Seeing her lying there he wasn't at all sure he could do what his plan would require of him. Even if he'd been right and sticking to the plan was the only way he'd be protected. He just wasn't sure he could do it.

He went to the sink and leaned over it to splash cold water on his face. He had to clear his head. After drying his face he stood straight up and raked his hand through his thick dark hair. He looked at the supplies he had at the ready. The taste of bile rose in his throat as he tried to talk himself into taking action. Now that he'd brought her here he had to finish what he'd started. The sooner he did it the sooner he could dispose of her body and move on. There's no turning back now, he told himself. And that's when he heard her soft moan. His head spun around in her direction. She'd woken up and was just realizing her hands were bound. She was confused and struggling.

The chloroform wasn't supposed to wear off this quickly. His pulse began to race again. His anxiety level spiked as he noticed that she was speaking. It was very quiet but she was definitely speaking. Not wanting her to know he was there he crossed the room quietly until he was just close enough to hear what she was saying.

"I know you're here with me, Father. Thank you, Lord. You promised *never* to leave me or forsake me. Thank you for being here with me right now. *Wherever I am.* Whatever's happening - you're here," she struggled again and shook her head from side to side. "*I can't see*," she said panic rising in her voice. "And my hands are tied. God, I'm scared. *I'm so scared!* Please help me. I don't know where I am. I don't know who took me or why they've done this. Please protect me, God. Please *help me.*" She gasped and suppressed what he thought could only be a sob that was rising up from deep inside her.

"Dear heavenly Father, I need you. I need you now *more than I've ever* needed you!" she was crying now. "Don't leave me, God. Please give me wisdom and help me through this. Please keep me safe and protect me as only you can."

He stood looking at her, listening to her prayer and seeing her struggle through her fear. Through all of that she continued to call out to the God she so obviously trusted in. He felt sick inside. As she continued praying he couldn't take it. He didn't want to see or hear her anymore. He had to get away from her. Without realizing what he was doing he took a step backward. He almost fell but caught himself.

"*Who's there?*" she shouted turning her head in his direction. "Who's there? Why have you brought me here? What do you want?"

He froze in place. This wasn't the way he'd planned it. It wasn't the way this was supposed to happen. *She shouldn't have come to.* He was going to kill her and leave her where no one would ever find her. No one ever came out here anymore. It was *the perfect plan.* He'd kill her and go on with his life. *That's all* he wanted. He just wanted to go on with his life.

"Are you there?" she asked quietly now, turning her head from side to side, trying to see.

"Oh dear Father, please show me what to do," she prayed again.

Turning in his direction again she raised her voice, "Please don't hurt me," she said. "I don't understand what's happening. I don't know what you want.

Please tell me what's happening. Please, just tell me what you want. If you'll tell me what you need I'll try to help you. We'll figure this out together. Oh, just please don't hurt me," she said as another sob caught in her throat.

He didn't know what to do now. Nothing was going according to plan. She seemed so kind. She was offering to help him, trying to be so brave. How could he kill this woman? He didn't even know her. He didn't really know what she knew or if it could even hurt him. He couldn't kill an innocent woman, *could he?*

Was that who he was now?

Seeing what he'd done he turned away from her in disgust. Trying to get away from her he rushed over to the kitchen counter. There he saw all the items he'd laid out. The instruments he was going to use to kill her. The plastic and the blanket he was going to wrap her dead body in. *Just thinking about it* was making him sick. *Physically sick.* Sick with self-loathing. Bile rose up in his throat. He couldn't stop it. *Oh no!!* He literally couldn't stop it. He turned quickly and vomited into the sink.

She heard what had happened and immediately began to pray. No longer in a whisper, no longer shouting. To his amazement she no longer even sounded afraid. Calmly, peacefully, in her normal speaking voice he heard her prayer as she lifted him up to God. She was praying *for him!* This woman who *he meant great harm to* was praying *for* him. He listened as she began asking God to help him. She begged God to turn him away from the evil that Satan had planned for his life - from the evil that he apparently had planned for her life. On and on, she prayed while he just stood there listening. He couldn't stop staring at her. Now she was asking God to open his eyes. To show him that whatever he'd planned to do wasn't right. It wasn't the answer. It wasn't going to help him. It would lead him to ruin and death. She was praying for his soul now. "Dear God, please lead this man to you. Help him turn to your son, Jesus. The only one who can set him free from the sin that so strongly binds him."

He couldn't bear to hear any more.

"*SHHHHH,*" he shushed her loudly. He couldn't let her hear his voice. He didn't want her to hear his voice but he *did want her to stop.* He *needed her to stop.* Compulsively, he rushed toward her still shushing her. "*SHHHHHHHHH*", he made the sound as loudly as he could, almost violently. His mouth was very close to her face now, "*SHHHHH*"

Realizing he'd rushed her, she drew back. She sensed his anger, his desperation. She stopped speaking. Her whole body was shaking from fear. He could clearly see that. But she'd stopped speaking and that was all that mattered to him in that moment.

He went back to the sink and washed away the vomit. Again he splashed cold water over his face sucking it into his mouth this time, swishing and spitting it out several times. He dried his face with the towel and stood looking at the instruments of evil he'd laid out in preparation. *"Instruments of evil"* his mind said to him as he stared at them. He hadn't thought of them that way until *just now*.

He was oblivious of her now. It was as if she wasn't even in the room anymore. He was lost in his own mind. All he knew was that he felt heartsick.

Defeated?

Weak?

Yes, but mostly just sick at heart.

He'd killed before but *that was different*. It was an accident. Victor had fallen. He'd hit his head and died. That wasn't the same as this. Yes, he'd hid the body. But he hadn't *murdered* Victor. If he killed this woman *it would be* murder.

I can't do this. He thought to himself. This isn't who I am. *This* isn't who *I want to be*.

As if she possessed an inherent wisdom telling her he needed this time to process what to do she sat perfectly still while he worked through it all. Arms bound behind her, eyes covered, gripped with fear to the core of her being.

He wasn't looking at her. If he had been he'd have seen that her lips were still moving. She continued silently calling out to God for his wisdom, his peace and his protection.

Forcing himself back to the matter at hand he looked in her direction again. He now knew what he had to do next.

CHAPTER 36

Vonda was *terrified*. She could hear him moving around in the room but she had no idea what he was doing. When she had first come to she'd been disoriented as she realized she couldn't see and her hands were bound. Then she remembered that someone had grabbed her. Her first instinct was to pray. So she prayed for herself and for this man, whoever he was. She'd talked with God just like she did every day of her life.

She had to believe now that God had led her to do that even though he was there and had been listening. She didn't know he was there at first. She *still* didn't know who he was. She had to assume he was a stranger but he'd never spoken so she didn't even really know that. She was amazed at the peace God was giving her despite her fear. And now she knew she needed to be silent. She instinctively understood that this man, whoever he was and whatever his plans, needed her to be silent.

She wouldn't stop praying though. He *couldn't make her stop praying*. She was trusting God to take care of her *no matter what* this man had planned. She'd just keep praying, silently, inside her mind.

She was listening intently, trying to figure out where they were or what he was doing. It sounded like he was moving tools around. Oh, dear heavens, what was he doing?

She couldn't get away. She couldn't even move her hands. The band was so tight she could feel it cutting into her skin any time she tried to move. She couldn't see. She couldn't see *at all*. Still, she was thankful the eye covering was soft and not so tight that it hurt her. It's important to be thankful, she thought. It was terrifying to be tied up and blindfolded. She felt so badly for anyone who had every experienced this. She was *so scared*! Tears filled and fell from her eyes only to soak into the soft cloth covering them. She just kept asking God to give her a calm spirit and protect her. When she couldn't pray anymore she just kept thinking "Help me, God. Please help me." She was powerless.

But she *refused to believe* God was.

He was relieved that she had finally stopped talking. Her praying had unnerved him. *Who does that?* He kept glancing over at her to make sure she wasn't up to something while he gathered everything he had brought with him. He left her alone just long enough to put it all into the trunk of his car.

Finally, he wiped everything down. There would be nothing to prove he had ever been here. Not that he thought anyone would check this place. He took one long, last look around before setting his plan in motion. He wanted *nothing more* than to *end* this terrible night.

He wasn't sure if she heard or felt him approaching her but he knew she knew he was coming. Her body stiffened as she blindly prepared to fight him. He wanted to tell her not to fight but he couldn't let her hear his voice. She couldn't know anything about him.

He hated what he was about to do but he had no choice. There was just no other way.

As quietly as possible he prepared the cloth just as he'd done before. This time instead of enclosing it in a zip lock bag for later he placed it in the palm of his hand. He then moved as silently as possible toward her. She was sitting on the couch on high alert. Not having spoken a word since he'd shushed her earlier.

She sensed him coming so he rushed directly toward her. When she drew back from him in fear he quickly put the cloth over her mouth and nose. Just as he'd expected she tried to fight but with her hands bound behind her there was little she could do. The chloroform took effect more quickly this time. He scooped her up almost immediately, carried her out and placed her in the back of his car again.

As he drove through the night back to her house he tried to devise a plan. Again he killed the headlights until he pulled the car just off the road and into the woods behind her property. As silently as possible he retraced his steps, this time with her lying gently in his arms. If he remembered correctly she'd gotten her front door unlocked before he'd taken her. He hadn't meant to let that happen and was surprised he hadn't heard the alarm sounding as he'd whisked her away through the back yard. He could only assume it hadn't been set. He had thought luck was on his side earlier. He now realized that if he was right and the door was unlocked it would mean luck was on his side *now*. He reached out and turned the doorknob gently. *Yes!* It gave and the door opened. The second he was inside he turned quickly to find the alarm box just inside her door. Relieved to see it wasn't set he marveled at his good fortune. Unsure of what to do with her he walked straight ahead until he found her living room. He took her to the recliner and placed her in it. Hearing a deep, guttural, growl, he slowly turned to see a large white cat. Its long hair was standing up down the center of it back. Its back was hunched as it continued the low, hateful, growling. He'd never seen a cat do that before. Thankfully, it didn't appear it would actually attack him.

He turned back to the recliner and moved her just enough to cut the band from her wrists. Seeing the sore markings left there he felt deep sorrow. He gently laid her hands across her lap and placed her Bible on the table beside her chair. Seeing a cover in the large basket beside the chair he picked it up and spread it over her still form. He left her purse in its place. He'd been positive she was unconscious but had left the blind fold on until this, *the very last moment*. Feeling like the intruder he was he tried not to even look around the room as he hurriedly took the covering from her eyes. He noticed it was wet as he rushed out of her house. He couldn't lock the deadbolt but he took a few seconds to lock the doorknob. At least now she's safe inside her home, he thought. The next thing he knew he was running across her back yard & through the wooded area. Running so fast he felt like he was flying. He wanted nothing more than to be away from her, away from there, away from the man he'd *almost* let himself become.

CHAPTER 37

As Vonda came awake she felt disoriented. Feeling drugged she dragged her eyes open. She was deeply relieved not to be blindfolded. Slowly looking around she saw that she was safe in her own home. She was in her recliner.

Her nightmare was over! Had it all been a dream? A *very bad dream* of being blindfolded with her hands bound behind her. No, it was real. Wasn't it? It had *seemed so real*. Relief was slowly flowing through her body.

Seeing Lilly lying on the throw that covered her she brought her hands out from under it and reached to gather her cat into her arms. She stopped abruptly, startled to see the swollen red welts on her wrists. It *had* been real! *It did happen* - just as she remembered it.

Staring at her wrists her heart began to race as the terrifying memories flooded over her. Fear threatened to overtake her. Was he here? Was he with her in her house right now? Frantically, she jerked her head from side to side searching the open living area around her. Seeing no one she got out of her chair as quietly as possible and began sneaking around *in her own house.* Terrified he was going to appear at any moment. But wait, he'd kept her blind folded. He hadn't spoken. He didn't want her to see or hear him. She wasn't blindfolded or bound now. *He must not be here with her.* This was so confusing. What had happened? What in the world was happening to her? She was shaken to her core but a little less frightened as she walked all through her house and ensured that she was, indeed, there all alone.

Returning to the living room she saw her purse in the large basket where she usually kept the throw cover she used in her recliner. The cover he had obviously placed over her when he brought her back home. She picked up her purse, got her phone from it and immediately called the police.

Nothing made any sense. Why had he taken her? Why her and even more confusing why did he bring her back home? What had he planned to do and why didn't he? Was it because of her prayers? All she could say to that possibility was 'Thank you, Jesus!' She prayed for the man again right then, in the present moment. She asked God again to help him turn away from the evil he was apparently prone to, to save him from that life. But then fear stepped in again. What if he changed his mind? *What if he came back to take her again?*

Thinking about that Vonda walked outside and stood looking at the front of her house. He must've hidden behind the tall hedges on either side of her entryway. *She'd walked right past him* with *no clue* he was even there. That's how he'd come up behind her while she'd fumbled with her belongings and unlocked the house. She could see so clearly now *how easy* it had been for him.

She went immediately back inside picked up her phone and called the landscaping company she regularly used. By the time she hung up 5 minutes later they were scheduled to come to her house the next morning. By this time tomorrow the hedges would be gone from the front of her house. *Vonda would never be taken like that again.*

The officers arrived and took her statement of all that had happened. They then checked the house and property. They found nothing amiss but agreed it would be wise to have the front hedges shortened, if not completely removed.

They may've thought her crazy but for the marks on her wrist and the urgency with which she pronounced the truth of what she was telling them. They agreed with Vonda that the entire scenario made no sense. They told her she was one lucky woman. Vonda didn't believe it was luck at all. She felt sure God's protection over her was the only reason she was alive to tell her story.

The police insisted she go to the hospital to be checked out and submit a medical report to go along with theirs. She didn't think it necessary but ultimately agreed in the hope it could be medically proven he'd used chloroform to knock her out. That would be another confirmation that she was telling the truth.

To say the least, with the visit from the police and her trip to the hospital, it wasn't a pleasant morning.

CHAPTER 38

Vonda made herself a sandwich for lunch and then snuggled up in her recliner with Lilly in hopes of taking a long nap. She didn't feel up to much today. It was so odd to think of her captor returning her to her home, placing her in her recliner and even covering her up the way he'd done. He'd placed her purse in the basket where he'd gotten her cover and even laid her Bible on the stand beside her. *What kind of criminal does that?*

This was all so confusing. No matter how many times she went over it in her mind she couldn't make sense of it. Still feeling shaky and out of sorts she just kept thanking God she was safe. She felt exhausted but wasn't at all sure she'd be able to sleep. She found herself just sitting there staring. Finally, her eyes became heavy and she fell into a deep sleep.

When she woke up several hours later she felt better. She wasn't her usual self, by any means, but she felt steadier and a little surer of herself.

Realizing it was Thursday she decided not to let this situation deter her from her usual activities. After a small supper she got ready to walk to the ball field. She debated driving but, again, refusing to give this man the power to change her life she stuck to her usual routine. Being sure she set the house alarm before setting out she wondered if she'd ever forget to set that again. She'd forgotten more than a few times recently. Last night had been one of them. The other thing she did was make sure she carried her pepper spray. She'd forgotten that on many occasions when she'd gone out to walk. She felt quite confident she wouldn't be forgetting that anymore either. Nothing like a simple abduction to snap you into focus on safety issues, she thought, while walking to the ball park.

Half an hour later as she sat in the stands watching the fellows warm up she was glad she'd come. *This was good.* There was a sense of normalcy. It felt good being in a familiar place, a pleasant place. Yes, this was definitely good for her. It was helping her get her bearings back.

As the evening wore on she concentrated on watching the game. Paying attention to which players were there, cheering, and chatting with those around her as she did each week. There were even a few moments when she forgot about what had happened and actually began to enjoy herself. Granted those moments were *very few and very brief* but they *did* happen.

As was her habit each week she stayed behind chatting with Marshall as he gathered up the bases, bats and baseballs and put them away. She would sometimes help him carry them over to the equipment house where he'd lock them safely away.

Marshall noticed she seemed a little quiet this evening. Not quite as chatty as usual. As they moved along together they both suddenly leaned forward and reached for the same bat at the same time. Realizing what was happening they laughed until Marshall noticed the welts on her wrist where the long sleeved shirt she'd chosen to wear this evening had ridden upward.

"What in the world happened?" he asked with concern as he reached for her hand and caught it in his. Vonda cried out quietly. Realizing he'd unintentionally hurt her Marshall released her hand immediately. He took her shoulders in his hands gently and began profusely apologizing.

"It's all right. It's all right!" Vonda said looking him directly in the eyes. "You didn't know. You had no way of knowing. It's all right. I'm fine now."

"What happened to you?" Marshall's voice was full of concern as she pushed the shirt sleeve up and allowed him a better look at her injuries.

"It's kind of a long and terrifying story," she said with a slight catch in her voice. "Let's get the rest of this put away and if you'll drive me home I'll tell you all about it."

"Of course," he answered. "Of course, but you let me do this. You're not picking *anything* else up tonight."

She nodded her agreement and began to tell him what had happened the previous night. By the time they arrived at her house Marshall had gotten the bulk of the story. He was as confused as she was at the circumstances she had described.

On the few past occasions when the game had run past dark and Marshall had driven her home he'd always insisted on walking her to the front door and seeing her safely inside. It wasn't even dark yet but Marshall insisted she let him go in with her and check out the house before leaving. Even though she knew she had set the alarm code this time Vonda agreed. She wasn't too proud to admit to being afraid. It was comforting to have him come in with her.

Once they were inside Marshall waited as Vonda entered the code to disarm the security system. Vonda then invited him to stay and visit with her a while and he gladly accepted.

CHAPTER 39

Marshall complimented Vonda's home as she made them each a warm mug of apple cider. They sat down at her dining room table and continued talking about her harrowing experience of the night before.

"You know, it sounds ridiculous to say this, but I'm actually thankful for these injuries on my wrists," Vonda told him. "I'm not sure the police would've even believed me if it weren't for them."

"I can see what you mean," Marshall answered. "Without that to substantiate your story it's almost unbelievable. I mean, why would someone abduct you, keep you blindfolded and bound in some obscure location for several hours without actually harming you. I'm sorry, I realize *everything* he did was harmful but you know what I mean, right?" She nodded her agreement and he continued, "Only to chloroform you again and return you to your home while you were knocked out. It makes absolutely no sense."

"And yet, that's *exactly* what happened," Vonda said shaking her head in confusion.

They sat silently sipping their cider for at least a full moment. Vonda sat at the table facing in the direction of the sliders while Marshall sat facing her.

Lost in thought Vonda softly said "I don't understand why these senseless things are happening to me."

"What d'ya mean? What else has happened?"

"Well, I can't help thinking of the night I couldn't sleep. It's been quite a while ago now. Sometimes I get hit with a wave of grief. I don't know how else to explain it. It was during one of those times. I'd been grieving for a few days that week and on this particular day, as will sometimes happen with grief or depression, you just want to sleep. So I'd slept too much during the day and woke up well into the evening. Of course, that left me awake during the night. I'd woken back up well after dark, maybe around 10:30 or so and I sat reading for a while. About midnight I realized I'd never shut the blinds. Those" she said, pointing to her large picture window "or those." She added as she pointed to the blinds for the sliders. "Not wanting to get up I just sat here in the dark looking out the window. That's when I noticed this strange repetitive light. It was very curious and I couldn't quite figure out what it was. My curiosity got the best of me so I opened the sliders and stepped out onto my patio. And that's when I realized there was a repetitive sound taking place, too. That's what I meant when I said 'senseless things keep happening.' I mean granted, this is nothing like being abducted and returned but still it makes no sense. It's even strange, right?"

"Well, it does sound strange. Is that all there was to it, just a strange light? What kind of sound was it?"

"It was kind of a scrapping and then a clunk. I don't know, like something was being dropped. Yes, like that, I guess. Something was being scrapped along the ground and then dropped. Anyway, it only went on for about two minutes once I opened the slider. I realized the sounds had stopped and then after about twenty seconds I realized the repetitive light had gone away, too. So I came back inside."

So where was this light you were seeing? I mean, it's dark right now. Just like that night, right? So point out where you were seeing it," Marshall got up from the table and started toward the picture window.

"No, not that way," she stopped him. "Yes, I was sitting in my recliner but I was looking this way toward the sliders, not toward the picture window. Like this, see?" She sat in the recliner and demonstrated by leaning to the right in a reclined position so that she was actually looking off to the side of her chair toward the sliders.

She got up then and both of them walked to the sliders. She pulled the shades back and pointed toward the house, which at the time had been a part of the new construction and wasn't being lived in yet.

"That house?" Marshall asked pointing to the correct house and then turning to look at her.

"Yes, that's the one," she nodded up at him. "It was a new construction at the time. The new owners hadn't moved into it yet but it was almost finished."

"We built that house," Marshall said. "It's one of ours. My company, I mean, Davidson Construction. That house is part of the Hardee Street Project. It's one of our biggest current projects."

"Really?" Vonda asked incredulously. "Your Company's the one doing all the building right here in my neighborhood? I hadn't realized that. That's really something." She smiled at him.

"Well, not all of it is us, no. But Hardee Street is. We're building all the new homes going up on Hardee Street. So, what you're telling me is that something strange was going on at one of my building sites after midnight. Now *I'm* curious. In fact, I'm *more than curious*. None of my crew should *ever* be on the job site at that hour. I'd like to know myself what was going on with this strange light and the sounds. That's all though, right. You didn't see anything else?"

"Well, not right then, no. But I remember there was a three quarter moon so the sky was pretty bright that night. It was just such a beautiful night, really. It was quiet and peaceful. Just the kind of night I enjoy so I stood here by the sliders taking it in for a little bit. Finally, maybe about ten minutes after I'd come back inside I reached up to shut the blinds. That's when I saw a truck with its headlights turned off driving in this direction. *I couldn't believe that.* I mean that's just dangerous. I actually watched for the driver to turn them back on for fear he'd hit something driving in the dark like that. I stood here, just like we are now and watched him drive all the way up the road with his lights off. Then he turned off onto the next road, right up there, see?" She pointed as she continued talking. "Just before he drove out of sight I saw the headlights come on. I was *so relieved* to see that."

Closing the blinds on the sliders Vonda motioned to the living room furniture. Marshall went over and got comfortable on her couch as she took his empty mug from the table and put it, along with hers, into the dishwasher. She joined him in the living room.

"I have to agree with you, Vonda. That all sounds very strange. Being as it took place at one of my building sites I feel a bit of a responsibility to know what was going on. You wouldn't happen to know what night this happened, would you?"

"Oh, Marshall, I don't," she said, shaking her head sadly. "I might've made note of it if everything hadn't been back to normal the next day. But it was just fine. Like I said, I was up half the night that night so I slept in later than usual the next morning. By the time I got out on the patio and settled in my rocking chair to enjoy my coffee there was just a flurry of activity over there. I purposely looked. I mean I do that most mornings anyway. I enjoy watching the homes go up. But that particular morning I wanted to be sure everything was okay.

Oh, wait. I *do remember* what was going on that day. That's right, I remember now. The cement truck was there. That was the day the new driveway was poured."

CHAPTER 40

On the drive home Mason was amazed at how enlightening these Greif Share sessions were for him. He felt very thankful he'd decided to make this thirteen week commitment. Now that he understood what it was all about he believed wholeheartedly this was going to improve his life. It seemed to him that his eyes were opened to something new each week and as soon as he saw it he was able to change it. Making those changes *felt really good.*

Hearing the others share how the death of their loved ones had impacted them was helping him, too. He'd never really given much thought to grief or what it meant or how it worked. He definitely never realized before this how important it is to allow oneself to grieve. Through the DVD's they'd watched, the workbook and the group discussions he'd come to realized grief is a very personal experience. It's unique to each person. Yet, at the same time it causes similar reactions and behaviors in most people. He was definitely finding it helpful to realize that much of what he'd felt and thought immediately following his parents deaths were normal reactions to grief.

Looking back on it now he was amazed at how much he'd shut himself off from life without even realizing it. He remembered feeling numb in those early days and sometimes feeling like he was going crazy. What a relief it was to hear many others share having those same thoughts and feelings.

The more he learned about the grief process and about himself the lighter and happier he felt but for one thing, that *one terrible thing.* That thing that happened which he could never tell anyone about. He'd come a long way in trusting Dr. Rossman but he was afraid to tell her, or anyone else, what he'd done. Anyone who knew about it would see him differently. Not to mention the legalities involved if it were ever to become public knowledge. No, it had to stay his secret, his alone.

It was a *terrible* burden but one he knew he must carry for the rest of his life. He was appalled at himself. Not only for what he'd done but for the lengths he'd gone to cover it up. He *couldn't forgive himself.* And if he couldn't forgive himself how could he expect forgiveness from anyone else? This was one secret he was just going to have to live with.

Still, he didn't want it to be his undoing. He was determined *not* to let that happen. He had to find a way to live with what he'd done and still continue rebuilding his life.

Rebuilding his life, that's what he was trying to do by taking counseling and attending Grief Share and *it was working*. With each passing week he was more convinced it was helping him become a better man. And he felt grateful.

Although he still didn't quite understand why - he'd come to realize he was prone to frustration. And that anger had always been his go-to emotion. He could also see that the behavior those emotions led him to wasn't doing him any favors. Most of the problems he'd had were a result of a poor choice he made in a moment of anger.

If only he'd taken counseling and found a Grief Share group earlier in his life. He was certain that what happened that fateful night never would've happened. But it *did happen* and it couldn't be undone now. As sad as that was, there was no point in letting it stop him from changing his behavior from this point on.

He could see healing and growth taking place in his life. He could see the difference these sessions were making and *he liked it*. He truly felt that by continuing with the Grief Share sessions he'd be able to find the underlying reason for his anger and frustration. And once he knew that he could learn to be free of them.

He truly believed that! In fact, he was counting on it!

He wanted *nothing more* than to be free of those emotions and the behaviors they brought out in him. If he could accomplish that he was certain Stacey would never have a reason to be afraid of him again. *They could be a family again*. That was all *he'd ever* wanted and it was all he wanted still.

CHAPTER 41

With the first of the Hardee Street homes now completed the construction crews had started on the next two, which were basically going up simultaneously. The foundations had been laid and the houses had both been framed in. The interior walls were now standing and the wiring and plumbing had been run. The walls were ready for drywall.

In the early years the company only did residential homes with Manny and Saul as crew leaders. Years later Saul led the crew on the first commercial project they'd taken on while Manny stayed with the residential projects. That worked out well so they'd continued on in that manner. The company was growing fast and getting more projects in both venues. It still averaged more residential than commercial buildings.

At last month's meeting of Marshall and the two crew leaders the topic of hiring another crew leader was broached. Manny insisted it wasn't necessary. He could supervise two crews simultaneously. The other two agreed to operate on that basis for a while to see how it worked out. They'd all agreed that if Manny became overwhelmed they'd approach Mitch about becoming a crew leader. Today Manny had both crews working the Hardee Street Projects. Saul and his crew were working the commercial project currently taking place in downtown Stokesbury.

Manny and his crews had been hard at it hanging drywall all morning. Manny got a call that he was needed for an emergency board meeting at Corporate. He hurriedly let the crews know he was taking off. While heading out the door he called out "Mitch, please take over, as usual. Everyone, please defer to Mitch. Most likely I won't be available the rest of the day." And he was gone. The crews were fairly self-sufficient so they continued working as normal.

Mitch had been at it alone for quite a while when Carlos joined him asking if he could use an extra set of hands. While it *can be done* hanging full drywall sheets is awkward for one man so Mitch readily agreed. It was usually easier and almost always more enjoyable working together as opposed to working alone. There was generally no discussion but at times co-workers chatted about current events or local political issues while working side by side. Today was no different until things took a more personal turn.

While hanging a new sheet of drywall Carlos casually commented on how much easier the job was with more hands on deck. Mitch agreed and Carlos began to talk about not understanding why he wasn't getting scheduled for more work. With all the current projects going it certainly seemed as if the work was available. Carlos refreshed Mitch's memory that he'd come on board on a part-time basis six months ago. He again lamented that he still hadn't been asked to join full-time. He was trying to be patient but his girlfriend had recently moved in and now they were furnishing his place. He went on to say that with the added expenses he'd recently taken on a second part-time job and was now working at El Campestre.

Mitch had just been listening as Carlos chattered on.

At this point Carlos said he was a little nervous because Marshall had recently come into the restaurant when he was working. Carlos wasn't sure but thought Marshall might've seen him serving tables.

"Why is that a problem?" Mitch asked. "Nothing says you aren't free to work a second job. Even if Marshall did see you, it's not a problem."

"No?" Carlos asked. "Are you sure? I don't want to jeopardize my job here. I wish they'd just give me more hours."

"Have you talked with Manny about it?" Mitch asked him.

"I haven't," Carlos admitted. "I mean, Manny's my uncle. I don't want it to seem like I'm asking favors because I'm family."

"He's also your crew leader," Mitch answered him straightforwardly. "He's the one you have to go to if you want more hours, more pay, time off, whatever. You can't let his being your uncle stop you from doing what you need to do to get what you need from this job."

"I guess that makes sense," Carlos answered. "I suppose that's what you've done, since you're family to the boss?" Mitch didn't answer and he went on, "Well, thanks for the advice. I'll have to ask Manny if there's a reason they're keeping me at part-time and tell him I want more hours."

"Yep, I'd say that's what you need to do," Mitch answered.

CHAPTER 42

"Do they have anything to go on at all?" Manny asked of Marshall as he and Saul entered the small conference room. The three were scheduled to meet with Lead Detective Andrew Wood who was heading up the investigation into Victor Tonnae's recent disappearance.

"If I'm not mistaken that's what he's coming to talk with us about," Marshall commented. "But to answer your question, I really have no idea. I know they've talked with everyone who saw and talked with Victor on the last day he was at work. The detective mentioned hoping we could be of assistance. Of course, I said we'll do all we can. I just don't know what that would be."

There was a gentle knock and all three men turned toward the door to see DeeDee standing there with Detective Wood. DeeDee motioned him into the room. After being sure there was nothing else they needed of her she left, closing the door behind her. The detective shook Marshall's hand and thanked him for agreeing to the meeting. Marshall, in turn, reminded the detective of who his two businesses partners were. He wasn't sure if they'd actually met when the detective had addressed all of the staff in regard to Victor's disappearance. After handshakes all around, they each took a seat.

"Thank you for agreeing to meet with me today," Detective Wood said. "I want to fill you in on how the investigation into Mr. Tonnae's disappearance is going. Then I'll explain where I'm hoping you can be of help."

"Sounds good," Marshall responded. The other two men nodded their heads in agreement.

"I'll be honest. This case has got me stumped," Detective Wood said. "It's like the man disappeared off the face of the earth, for no apparent reason, without leaving a trace. Everyone we've talked to who saw or talked with him that last day have basically said the same thing. He was intent on going home, finishing his packing and heading off for vacation the next morning. He was excited about the trip. He gave no one any indication of second guessing himself, cancelling the trip or having any other plans. He didn't mention detouring for any stops on his way home. He said nothing to anyone indicating the possibility that he wouldn't go or that there was anything else on his mind. We've also talked with his neighbors and landlord. No one there has given us anything new to go on.

A thorough search of his apartment and his neighbor's testimonies indicate that most likely he never made it home. His luggage was partially packed. But all of the things you'd put in right before heading to the airport, you know, toiletries, last minute items, were never added. The plane ticket and his vacation itinerary were laid out side by side on his dining room table. Everything was at the ready. If he'd gone home all of that should've been in his vehicle when it was found. The only thing found there was his briefcase, which of course, we conclude he was simply taking home from the office.

From the interviews with your staff it appears your Office Manager DeeDee was the last one to speak with him. She mentioned that he'd gone into a file room. I think she called it the Vendor File room, not long before she left for the day. He was in his office still looking over paperwork when she relayed her good wishes for his vacation, told him goodnight and left.

So, gentlemen, here's where you come in, we've done a search of his office here and of the briefcase. Obviously, none of our detectives are accountants. So the amount of paperwork and the specific documents an accountant would normally carry in his briefcase aren't details we're clear on. I've looked at the contents and truthfully, it doesn't seem like much of anything to me and certainly nothing unusual. But this isn't my area of expertise. I'm hoping one, if not *all of you*, will be willing to come down to the station to the evidence locker with me to look over the contents of his briefcase and offer your input."

The three looked at each other and without needing to confer each one knew that, of course, they'd do all they could to help locate Victor.

"I'd also like to request, Mr. Davidson that you, or a person of your choosing, go through Mr. Tonnae's desk. Just to see if anything surfaces that gives an indication of something amiss. Perhaps a hint of something that could've been going on that may've led to his disappearance."

Although no one could imagine what that might be Marshall agreed to look Victor's desk over at his earliest convenience. The men then headed out to meet Detective Wood at the Police Station.

CHAPTER 43

Waking up on Friday morning Vonda could only hope for a normal day. It had been a restless night. She imagined that was to be expected after one was abducted. The more focused she became as she woke up the more thankful she was to be safe in her own bed in her own home. She was reminded of how much we take for granted on any given day.

Heaven only knew what could've happened to her and why it didn't. She felt grateful and repeatedly thanked God the whole ordeal was over.

As she moved through her morning routine her thoughts returned to her visit with Marshall last evening. He'd been astonished to hear of her experience, of course. He was also very interested in whatever was going on at the new house on Hardee Street the night before the driveway was poured. What a surprise for her to find out Marshall's company was building the new homes. Thankfully, she'd remembered about the driveway being poured. That would give him a time reference. She couldn't imagine how he could figure out what had been going on that night. She really hadn't seen anything that made any sense, but she hoped he could. Marshall had been very thoughtful throughout the rest of their visit.

Well, she'd definitely given him a lot to think about with her bazaar tales.

Coffee in hand Vonda opened the sliders and stepped out onto the back patio and sank into her rocking chair. As she savored the first sip of coffee she noticed a movement at the Hardee Street house. It was the new owner, Ivy, coming out her front door. Vonda watched as she walked down the driveway and retrieved the newspaper from the paper box and returned inside. She had met Ivy and Dan not long after they'd moved into their new house. They hadn't spent any time together but they now regularly waved and smiled whenever they passed each other. Vonda often prayed for them while sitting out back in the mornings. She also prayed for the construction team. Until her conversation with Marshall last evening she'd had no idea she was actually praying for the crew of her new friend's business. What a reminder of what a small world it really is.

Remembering her earlier promise to pray for Marshall and his two brothers she took a few minutes to ask God to work in each of their lives in whatever way was needed. Mason in his marriage and the counseling he was taking. Marshall with all the business responsibilities he shouldered each day.

Not actually having met Mitch yet she just asked God to be with him in whatever he might need. She specifically asked God to help each of the brothers find their way back to the faith their young parents were raising them with when they so tragically died. She admitted to not knowing what the men needed. She knew God did so she simply asked Him to provide whatever would best help them in their daily lives. She prayed for each man to have the happy and fulfilling life she knew God wanted for them.

At the same time Vonda was enjoying her time on the deck Marshall was feeling frustrated in his office. He'd been distracted all morning. He just couldn't seem to focus on anything at work when there were serious issues happening elsewhere. From the day the police had come to him with the news of Victor's mysterious disappearance he'd been distracted. Having them search Victor's office and interview staff had only added to it. Victor was a vital employee to the company but, not only that, over the past year he'd become a trusted friend.

Marshall liked Victor from the first moment they met. He was drawn to Victor's attitude. His willingness to move across country for a new career opportunity appealed to Marshall. Based on his business credentials alone Marshall had been excited to have him join the company. It was an added bonus that from day one Victor had taken the initiative to learn everything he could to excel at the duties of his new position. He'd earned Marshall's respect on a professional level almost immediately.

Above that, Victor was likeable. His youthful energy, outgoing personality, good sense of humor and kindness were refreshing. He was exactly the kind of employee and person Marshall wanted in his company and his life. Marshall was *very troubled* over his disappearance. He actually found himself praying the young man would be found safely and very soon. But this latest meeting with Detective Wood didn't make that sound likely. The trip to the station he and his partners had made to look through the brief case hadn't yielded any new leads. Marshall didn't hold much hope of finding anything revealing when he looked through Victor's desk either. What in the world could've become of him?

As if all of that weren't enough of a distraction Marshall had now learned of Vonda's recent abduction which made absolutely *no sense*. Why would a woman be taken out of her home with the obvious intent of impending harm only to be returned unharmed the same night? It was mindboggling to say the least. He was equally troubled to learn about her noticing strange activity at the first new home Davidson Construction had built on Hardee Street. And in the middle of the night! Marshall felt as if his brain had been overloaded with information. Truthfully, he had no idea what to focus on first.

CHAPTER 44

Stacey Davidson sat awkwardly on the pine green, leather couch in Dr. Rossman's office. On the opposite end of the couch sat her husband, Mason. The two hadn't lived together for the past twenty weeks and their interactions had centered only on their two sons. When Mason invited Stacey to attend this therapy appointment with him he said it wasn't about her. He simply wanted to share some things he was learning about himself. It *wasn't* an attempt to get her to let him move back home.

Dr. Rossman entered the room, introduced herself to Stacey and welcomed Mason to the session. She then asked Mason to begin.

Mason turned toward his estranged wife on the couch beside him and thanked her for coming. He then continued, "I asked you to come today, Stacey, because I want to thank you for all the years you've spent with me. You're *still* the best thing that's *ever happened* to me. I know I haven't told you that a lot through the years. But it's *so true*."

He went on to admit knowing that their relationship hadn't always been easy for her and had, in fact, been quite difficult sometimes. He reminded her of how they used to talk intimately about their deepest thoughts and feelings. He acknowledged that somewhere along the way that had changed. He apologized for allowing the distance that had settled between them.

Stacey sat quietly giving him her full attention, taking everything in. Mason went on to share that while she'd often referred to his frustration and anger he'd never really gotten it. He just didn't see that in himself. His was a carefree attitude and fun personality. Stacey smiled and nodded her agreement. She couldn't deny that those were very real parts of the man she'd fallen in love with and stayed with through thick and thin over the years.

Finally, Mason revisited the incident that had caused Stacey to insist that he move out of their home. He shared his inability to comprehend how she could feel such fear of him that she'd draw back the way she had. Tears formed in her eyes as the memory was brought fresh to her mind. Tears formed in his eyes as he assured her he was *incapable of ever* hurting her. After a brief and hesitant hug between them Mason went on to admit the reason he couldn't believe she feared him was that he didn't see his anger the way she did.

During all the years she'd loved him and lived with him she had seen the internal struggle that raged inside him and how the anger teetered on the edge. Through all those same years he *hadn't seen it*. He'd shoved it deep down and every time it tried to resurface he denied it and refused to face it. He had buried it so deeply he couldn't see it even when it kept pushing its way back to the surface. He invited her here today to share that seeing her fear of him had forced him to take a look at himself in ways he didn't want to.

"I love you, Stace," Mason said simply. "You and the boys are *everything to me*. There's *nothing* I wouldn't do for you. That being true I've finally taken your advice and sought help. Dr. Rossman and I have been doing some hard work. She's been helping me figure things out. She's taught me to identify emotions, face the past and allow myself to remember things I didn't want to think about. She even encouraged me to attend a Grief Share group. I've been going and I just can't believe what's come from it. I had no idea but for all these years I've needed to grieve for my mom and dad. I needed to let myself remember them and face things I've put out of my mind for far too long. That's why I've asked you here today. You're the reason I'm learning all of this and learning it will help me heal. *Thank you, Stacey* for loving me all these years, even when I've been unlovable. No, *especially then*! Thank you for pushing me to get the help I've needed. Thank you, most of all that you've *never stopped loving me*." There was a catch in his throat as he said that. "The only reason we're here today is that when you told me you needed space and time away from me you said you still loved me and you wanted us to work this out. I hope and pray with everything in me that that's still true."

Stacey nodded her head ever so slightly giving him the hope he so desperately wanted and needed.

CHAPTER 45

Mason looked at Dr. Rossman who smiled a faint smile. She gently nodded her head encouraging him to continue.

"I've learned so much about myself," Mason said. "And I'm excited to share all of it with you. But right now I'm only gonna tell you what you really need to know. *You were right,* Stacey. I've been angry. I didn't know why I was angry so I just kept denying it. It's kind of crazy how these things go. Recently, I've been able to look at things I haven't looked at in years. Once I started doing that I started remembering things I hadn't thought about in years. From there things started to fall into place in a way they really needed to. I want to tell you all about that. Is that okay with you?"

Stacey leaned toward him, looked him directly in the eyes and said, "Yes, Mason, I want that very much."

He shifted his position on the couch and looked down at his hands as they rested on his knees. He lifted his head and looked her in the eyes. He took a deep breath and began to tell her about the relationship he'd had with his parents as he grew up, the love he felt from and for them. He talked about becoming a teenager and beginning to separate himself from them, as all children do, at a certain age. He talked about his growing pains and how they had affected his parents. He shared his remembrance of arguments they began to have as he exerted his desire not to go to the church youth group anymore. He wasn't connecting with the kids at church and his parents didn't like that, especially his mom. The more she tried to push him in that direction the more he rebelled. They fell into a pattern of very heated arguments and the distance between them grew wider.

Stacey's heart broke for the man she loved as she thought about the boy he'd been. He went on to share that one day his mom was sitting in the swing that hung from the large oak tree not far from the driveway. Mason had just been dropped off at home after ball practice. Instead of walking past her like he usually did he sat down. They sat in silence gently swinging back and forth until his mom turned to him and said she was sorry. She was *so sorry* for the many fights they'd had lately. Mason immediately told her *he was the one* who was sorry. He'd behaved terribly. And just like that they began to talk openly and honestly with each other.

He told his mom he didn't fit in at church anymore. He told her she didn't understand how hard that was. She agreed, adding that she wanted to and she would try to. She told him she loved him and that no matter what she would always be there for him. That she'd help him in any way she could and they were going to get through this together. She knew he was growing up and she had to let that happen. She told him he was her little boy and it was hard for her to see him in any other way. But she knew she had to learn to let him grow up and become the man God had created him to be. She was working on it. She assured him that no matter how hard it was for them to get through this they'd figure it out. They would do it together.

Then she took his face in her hands and looked him dead in the eyes. She told him she loved him and promised him she would always be there for him *no matter what - for the rest of his life – she would be there.* She said that someday when he was a grown man, a husband and a father himself, they would look back on this day together. They'd be proud of themselves for how they had talked it out and worked through it and managed to love each other through all these growing pains.

The two of them had gotten up from the swing, hugged each other and walked into the house together. Mason had felt *such a sense of relief* that day. He believed everything was going to be alright.

Later that evening his parents had come to his bedroom together. They knocked on his door. He invited them in and his mom told Mason she'd filled his dad in on their talk. She had invited his father to make the same commitment and promises she'd earlier made to Mason. His dad had agreed. The three of them talked briefly and then Mason and his father stood up, shook hands like men and then hugged each other. The three of them entered into a group hug and told one another good night.

Mason had gone to sleep with a light heart that night, believing it was all going to work out just as his mother had said.

The next day his parents broke every promise they had made to him.

They died.

CHAPTER 46

The day after Vonda was abducted she had the landscaping in the front of her house totally redone. Gone were the tall hedges that once flanked either side of her front, recessed entry way. Now there stood two Lantana shrubs flowering in vibrant orange. The Lantana flower attracts butterflies. Its shrub reaches a maximum of four feet high with a spread of up to three feet. Vonda had often admired Lantana's so it was only natural its shrub would be her first choice with the need to change the landscaping.

She was determined that if she couldn't erase the memory of the horrible night of her abduction she would, at least, rise above it by continuing to live a happy life. Butterflies had always made her happy. She liked to believe that sometimes Stanley's spirit hovered around her in the form of a butterfly. Overall, she just loved the idea of butterflies fluttering around her home. For these reasons the Lantana bush had been the perfect replacement for the tall hedges that were removed.

The police had yet to determine who had abducted her or why. While it was upsetting to know the man was still out there she comforted herself with the fact that he'd returned her safely home. She could only trust there was a reason for that and that he now had no intentions of harming her.

Since she'd told Marshall everything she had been through he'd taken to calling every evening to be sure she was safely locked in for the night. After losing Stanley Vonda had gotten used to being independent, she didn't like feeling as if she needed to be watched over. And yet, it was reassuring to have such a protective friend after her frightening experience so she decided to allow it. At least, until her abductor was caught. Sadly, without much to go on it remained to be seen whether the police were going to be able to figure out who it was. Let alone, locate and arrest the culprit.

In an attempt to distract herself Vonda decided to entertain her new friends. To that end she planned a simple gathering in her home and invited all of the Old Timers ball team members, their few but faithful spectators and a few friends from her church family. She set the hours from one until four on a Saturday afternoon. Having it fall between lunch and dinner would allow her to serve a variety of appetizers and desserts along with a delicious fruit punch, iced tea and canned soda.

As soon as she mentioned this idea to Marshall he volunteered to play co-host since his ball team would be attending. The day of the big event Marshall arrived at noon and helped Vonda arrange for extra seating and set the food on her kitchen counter and table. Once everything was in place they chose some light background music and sat chatting pleasantly while they waited to greet the guests.

CHAPTER 47

From the moment he heard about Vonda's get together he'd been looking forward to attending. It was the perfect opportunity to see how she had been doing since the harrowing experience he'd put her through. He *did* feel quite badly for that. Being in attendance would place him more firmly in her friend zone, hopefully removing him from any future suspicion. He knew the chances were slim that it would be mentioned but he had the thought that he may overhear news on the investigation.

Over the past several weeks his life had continued as usual with no one being aware of his involvement in Victor's disappearance or Vonda's abduction.

Arriving for Vonda's gathering he immediately noticed the drastic change to the front of the home. Smart woman that one. No one would ever be able to hide unseen at her front entry again.

A couple of the other ball team members were just arriving so he waited to enter the house with them. The three of them were greeted by Marshall who led them into the living/dining area of Vonda's home. Marshall made the formal introductions. Vonda greeted each of them warmly and thanked them for coming. She then gave them her warmest smile as she pointed out the eating utensils and array of food and drinks to choose from. He quickly joined the lighthearted conversation and mingled with the other guests as they all enjoyed the variety of delicious foods.

As the afternoon progressed a variety of guests came and went. For the most part they congregated in small groups throughout the main living area. Each group was making pleasant conversation with sudden bursts of laughter now and then. He was enjoying himself and was in no hurry to leave.

Everyone had been having a good time for just over an hour when he noticed Vonda's large white cat peeking around one of the doorways. The cat gracefully entered the room. Walking quietly and calmly she went unnoticed. She was well into the area when one of the guests saw her and loudly commented on her beautiful white fur. Vonda overheard the remark and quickly spotted her beloved cat.

"Oh, Lilly," she said with a smile "you've decided to put in an appearance, have you?" Lilly proceeded to pass several groups of people only showing them the slightest interest as she approached the center of the room. She was approximately 3 feet from the chair where he sat watching her when the cat's eyes met his and her demeanor suddenly changed. She immediately planted her front paws firmly in front of her and arched her back severely. Rising up on the pads of her front feet and sticking her head out toward him in an almost grotesque manner just before letting out that same deep, guttural growl he'd heard from this same cat once before. There was no question about it - *the cat remembered him.*

After her initial comments to Lilly, Vonda had turned away and gotten involved in a casual conversation with several of her guests. She now turned wide-eyed toward the cat. She had *never* heard Lilly growl before. *What in the world was going on?*

The room had become totally silent except for Lilly's deep throated growling.

"What in the world?" Vonda said as she followed Lilly's intense glare to his face. Realizing her cat was basically threatening a guest she quickly said, "*I am so sorry!* I don't know what's come over her." Still glancing apologetically in his direction she quickly approached Lilly. "I've never seen her act this way before."

Despite Lilly's aggressive stance and loud growling she scooped her cat up and quickly carried her out of the room. Lilly's eyes never left his and the ferocious growling continued until he was completely out of her sight.

Several of the guests commented how strange that had been. A few others shared times they'd seen animals have similar and unexplainable reactions.

Returning to the room, Vonda went straight over to him and apologized outright even as she admitted to being perplexed by Lilly's behavior. She repeated that Lilly had never done such a thing before and she hoped he wasn't unnerved.

"She's hissed on a few occasions but it's usually been when she's gotten underfoot and someone's accidentally stepped on her tail," Vonda said with a laugh, trying to lighten the mood in the room.

Vonda was saying all the right things but truthfully she was feeling a bit concerned. She truly had *never* heard Lilly growl before and *couldn't begin to imagine* what would have caused her cat to react to someone that way. She just had *no idea* what could've provoked such a response. In fact, if she hadn't seen it herself Vonda simply *would not* have believed it had ever happened.

After assuring her it was nothing to be concerned over he changed the subject by asking about one of the appetizers. The rest of the gathering passed without incident. To his disappointment there was never any mention of her recent abduction or its investigation, nor the one into Victor's disappearance.

Several hours later, immediately after the last guest had taken leave, Vonda went to the guest room where she'd placed Lilly. She'd never had to remove Lilly from a gathering before and wanted to see how she was doing. Opening the door she found her pet resting comfortably on the bed.

Vonda gathered Lilly into her arms as she went to purring deeply. Vonda carried her back into the living room. She then told Marshall she didn't understand Lilly's reaction and that, truthfully, it was causing her a bit of concern. Marshall didn't say anything to Vonda but it was causing him a bit of concern, too. He hated to admit it but in all actuality it had him *very concerned*. He could only think of one very real reason for Lilly's reaction. Was it possible Lilly had seen the man before - right here in Vonda's own home? Perhaps when he'd meant Vonda harm?

He hated what he was thinking, especially in light of *who Lilly had reacted to*. Could it actually be possible he was the one who had abducted Marshall's sweet, new, friend? *No,* Marshall thought. *It was just unthinkable.* However, he *was thinking it* and the very thought was making him feel sick.

CHAPTER 48

Stacey sat perfectly still as she continued listening to her husband pour his heart out. The results of his personal counseling and attendance in the Grief Share program were *astonishing.*

Mason shared that immediately after the death of his parents his life became a whirlwind of activity but through it all he'd had no one he could talk to. Marshall getting awarded guardianship over his brothers took precedence over everything else. It was all any of them thought about. With a growing business Marshall had been working long hours. That didn't change when he moved back into the family home so the boys learned to fend for themselves. Marshall made some valiant efforts in the beginning to go above and beyond on the weekends by taking them to a skateboarding park or bowling. It was his effort to make up for his lack of presence during the week. Sadly, there was nothing he could've done that would've softened the blow of losing their parents.

Once the initial shock of all these changes wore off Mason quickly became consumed with anger. *How could they do this?* How could they promise they'd be there for him and then immediately *just leave him?* He couldn't wrap his mind around that at all.

In the weeks that followed the only thing that seemed to go right was that his guardian big brother never mentioned church and he never went back there. As the weeks passed Mason was thrilled to realize he'd been set free of the social awkwardness of his Sunday class and weekly youth group meeting and events. He was now free to pursue the friendships that suited him. This, in turn, created guilt feelings. How could he be so happy about getting his own way when it had come at the cost of his parents' lives? *How cold hearted was he, anyway?* At this point Mason was harboring not only his feelings of anger and guilt but of un-forgiveness. The more complicated his life became in those first couple of years the more he resented his parents for leaving him. On the rare occasions he let himself think about all of this he always came back to one very clear conclusion. *He would never forgive them.*

It didn't take long to figure out Marshall's main concern was getting the boys through school and out on their own.

Despite his best intentions Mason always seemed to end up in some kind of problem. He'd be accused of having an attitude in class or something he

135

said or did would be interpreted by his peers as a challenge. He then, *of course,* would have to defend his honor which always led to a fight. And every time it happened his big brother/legal guardian got called in to try to straighten it all out. It wasn't long before Marshall began to look at Mason with annoyance, which resulted in more guilt feelings, anger and frustration in Mason. It was a vicious circle.

As Stacey sat listening to her husband sharing all of this, she thought back to that time in his life. She'd been a year younger than him in school but was aware of who he was. In fact, she'd always thought he was cute. She used to try to get his attention whenever he was in her vicinity.

She clearly remembered the death of his parents. Most people in school at that time did. It was a huge tragedy which affected the entire community. It's not often that two of the town's people die in a horrible car accident on the same day, let alone two people in the same family. Stacey remembered watching Mason and Mitch whenever she was around them afterward. She was always wondering what they must be feeling. Her heart had gone out to them.

Mason had gotten to the part of the story where he was about to get closer to Stacey. She remembered this part of his life very well. It was when she'd fallen in love with him. Mason was fun and funny and an outrageous flirt. Stacey had loved his personality. They'd become physically involved very quickly and only six months later she'd discovered she was pregnant. They married quietly but she lost the baby a week later. She'd grieved heavily for that child but Mason had quickly moved on. She remembered feeling hurt and lonely at the time. She'd basically grieved alone but eventually they had moved on together. In those early years she would occasionally see Mason's temper flair up. She never liked it but was convinced love conquered all.

Mason skimmed over the early years of their marriage and into the later years when they were finally blessed with their sons. He recited specific instances when his frustration or temper was a problem. At the time he had blamed Stacey, other people, *just about anyone and anything* except himself. Now, he wanted to own it. For the first time in their relationship Mason *was owning* his own behavior. Stacey didn't know what to make of it. Occasionally she interjected trying to minimize it but Mason wouldn't hear of it.

"No!" He finally snapped at her. "This is the way it was. You *know* it's true, Stacey. *You lived it!* Then his voice softened immensely as he said. "You saw me at my worst and you loved me still," he said it with such a tenderness it tore at her heartstrings.

"I don't know how you did that, Stacey, but *I'm so grateful* you did."

He was right. She had always loved him above all else. She still did.

CHAPTER 49

As they entered the room Marshall motioned for Manny and Saul each to take an easy chair in the casual seating area of his office. He'd set the area up many years ago for this very reason. His office had a large mahogany desk by a huge picture window where he did his paperwork and took phone calls. In the far corner of the room there was another good sized window. Years ago, once the business had succeeded enough for furniture purchases, he'd ordered the four large, leather, high back chairs and heavy wooden coffee table that now filled that space. It was to be a meeting area specifically for these three. Truthfully, the fourth chair wasn't needed and had been ordered just to even the space out. It had rarely ever actually been used. He took his usual chair as the other two took theirs and Marshall poured three tall glasses of sweet tea and set them on the table.

Most commonly when the three men sat in those chairs drinking sweet tea it was after their monthly business meeting on a Friday afternoon. They'd relax and enjoy ending the week together. These three men had proven to be an excellent team of checks and balances for the business over all these years. Some awesome business decisions had been made and ventures started right in this room. Although Marshall was the sole owner of the company he considered Manny and Saul equal business partners and made sure their salaries reflected that fact. The three of them made all the business decisions for the company together. On a personal level the three men celebrated life joys, offered support through hardships and laughed the hours away in this very setting.

Manny, Saul and Marshall were business partners but even more, they were best friends, lifelong buddies from childhood, who'd been along for the ride throughout each other's lives. There wasn't much one didn't know about the others. Theirs were the epitome of lifetime friendships. Marshall was thankful to have these two men at his side. He didn't know if any of their childhood classmates had managed to remain friends like the three of them had. He suspected it was a rare accomplishment and felt blessed to be part of it.

For this meeting today, something felt off. It wasn't an after-the-business-meeting talk. It wasn't a Friday. It wasn't a casual meeting where old friends would reminisce and joke around.

It felt odd. It not only felt odd, it was odd.

As the moments passed with the men silently drinking their sweet tea a quiet settled over their spirits. As Marshall sat looking at his two best friends, it crossed his mind that these were men you could trust your life to. He instinctively knew he could turn to them for anything and they'd be there for him. He had no idea just how true that would soon prove to be.

Manny and Saul didn't know what this meeting was about. They did know that in his own time and in his own way Marshall would tell them.

A moment later Marshall began to talk, he started out briefly talking about their friendship. He then talked about their business and how successful it was proving to be for each of them. He talked about what a great year this had panned out to be with the various business projects and the recent successful company picnic. Company morale was at an all-time high except for the recent disappearance of Victor.

Manny and Saul knew Marshall was working toward something so they simply gave him the time and space he needed to get there. Marshall was talking now about his friendship with Vonda. As often happened in this setting the conversation was crossing back and forth between business and personal. Marshall mentioned Vonda's recent gathering for the ball team and asked if either of them had been in the room when her cat had reacted to one of the guests. Neither of them had, so Marshall filled them in.

He then went on to mention that he hadn't told them about a recent event in Vonda's life out of respect for her privacy but he now felt he needed to talk with them about it. He hadn't figured out specifically how yet, but he had the nagging feeling whatever was going on with her somehow had something to do with their company. He'd called this meeting today to bring the two of them up to speed. He felt strongly that they needed to put their heads together and try to unravel exactly what was happening. Whatever it was, he now suspected it had been going on for some time and apparently right under their noses.

By this point, Marshall had the full attention of his friends and business partners. Whatever could he be referring to? Marshall filled them in on the recent abduction and return of Vonda. He then told them someone had apparently been doing something around midnight at the first of the Hardee Street home sites just before its completion. At that point both men were beyond curious. They were, as Marshall himself now was, *very concerned*.

CHAPTER 50

Monday's were always incredibly busy at Davidson Construction so it was well into the afternoon before Marshall even remembered the detective's request that he take a look at Victor's desk. He didn't want to feel rushed when he did it so he debated when would be the best time. DeeDee came rushing in right then with an urgent look on her face. She quickly explained that she'd finally gotten through to the fellow he'd asked her to reach almost an hour ago. He was currently on hold on line one. Of course, Marshall took the call. By the time he'd gotten off the phone Victor's desk had been completely forgotten.

It wasn't until late that evening that he thought of it again.

That's it. He told himself. I'm going in early tomorrow to get it done before the craziness hits. The next morning he did exactly that. It felt strange to sit at another man's desk. Willing himself to take his time and be thorough Marshall sat looking over the items on top of the desk. He'd decided to deal with the items on top of the desk before he even considered opening the drawers.

Funny, how you can work with a person day in and day out and never give any thought to the items on their desk. Most of the items were work related but there were a few that were obviously personal. Picking up the heavy glass paperweight with the copper coins imbedded inside he made a mental note to inquire of Victor as to its significance once he'd returned. A deep sadness settled over him almost immediately as the thought that he may not return at all crossed his mind. He didn't like thinking something fatal had befallen their young accountant. But the longer it went without his return the more the grim thought took hold in Marshall's mind. What in the world had become of Victor?

Half an hour later Marshal focused on the sadness that had settled over him as he looked closely at each item on the outside of Victor's work space. It had stayed with him as he considered each item in Victor's desk drawers. Victor was obviously very organized. Why, anyone could sit down at that desk and begin working immediately. That's how well Victor kept it. Not only was nothing out of place but everything seemed to have a logical reason for where it was. Sadly, Marshall had noticed nothing so far out of the realm of normal that it may offer an explanation as to where Victor had gone or why.

It was like the detective said. Victor had vanished, simply disappeared from off the face of the earth for no apparent reason.

Fully satisfied he'd done justice to his promise of checking out the desk Marshall arose and walked along the edge of the desk toward the door of the office. Reaching the top left corner of the desk his eyes fell onto the flip calendar sitting there. He'd picked it up earlier and turned to the last day Victor had worked just before his disappearance. He'd seen nothing other than a smiley face and arrow indicating to turn to the next page. Doing so, he saw that Friday's page had a tiny sketch of an airplane with a small smiley face beside it and the words Adventurous Vacation Begins. Now instead of returning to those same dates Marshall randomly flipped through the previous pages. He noticed small notations and began to stop flipping the pages long enough to read what Victor had written.

All the notations seemed perfectly normal; lunch appointments were noted with a time, location and name. There were random one word notations, most of which further thought could explain. One note said simply "Vendor List Compilation" Marshall noted the date and continued on. To his surprise he noticed that same note about 6 weeks later on. He took out a small notebook and wrote those two dates and the notation down before continuing through the flip calendar. The same notation caught his eye again two months later. This time the notation was followed with the word Deadline and a date. Turning to that date he found the following notation "VL Completed!" followed by a small smiley face drawing. Continuing to flip through the dated pages Marshall came upon another Vendor notation - albeit a little different. The handwritten notation on that date said simply 'follow up on vendor". That notation was followed by two capital letters and a question mark. It looked like this WW - ?

"Huh," Marshall said to himself as he continued staring at the calendar page wondering what it meant. When he flipped through the remaining pages he realized that notation had been made exactly one week prior to the last day Victor had worked. It saddened him to realize, once again, that no one had heard from Victor since.

Marshall had listed the dates of each Vendor note he'd come upon on Victor's flip calendar. He now stood studying the list. He didn't know what it meant. But it was definitely worth looking into. It was at this point Marshall remembered the Detective saying DeeDee had mentioned Victor going into the Vendor File room on his last afternoon of work. What Vendor was Victor following up on and why? Marshall couldn't imagine this having anything to do with Victor's disappearance but his curiosity was definitely peaked. Besides which anything concerning a Vendor was important to the company. Whatever Victor had been looking into Marshall intended to find out.

CHAPTER 51

Manny wasn't feeling well. He was actually feeling a bit unnerved. It had been weeks since the announcement of Victor's disappearance and the police didn't seem to be making any headway at all. At Detective Wood's request the partners had taken a look at the briefcase but noticed nothing amiss. There was a certain amount of unrest among the staff, especially those at corporate who'd worked with Victor on a daily basis. It was just troubling. Thankfully, it didn't seem to be affecting morale among the construction crews. Victor being part of administration it made sense that his corporate coworkers would be more affected by his disappearance than the construction teams. The whole situation was just weighing on Manny's mind as he worked with his crew on the Hardee Street Project today.

Carlos still wasn't getting the amount of hours he wanted and needed from his position on the Construction crew. He'd been considering what to do all week and had finally decided he'd take Mitch's advice and ask Manny if they could have a meeting to talk a few things over. He'd chosen today as the day to do that. When he did it Manny put him off by saying something about it being a bad time right now and not being sure when he could manage it. Carlos felt dismissed and walked away mad.

Mitch saw it all happen. He'd noticed in the weeks since Victor went missing there seemed to be an increasing amount of stress in the corporate office. He wasn't at corporate real often but lately every time he had been there he'd seen the police coming and going. It seemed to him there was a lot of tension in the air every day these days. He was himself pretty curious as to what exactly was going on. He figured everyone else probably was, too. Did the police have any leads? Were they finding new information or actual evidence or were they just continuing to question people who'd interacted with Victor on his last day? No one Mitch interacted with seemed to really know anything. As with all companies whenever something was out of the ordinary there were a certain amount of rumors floating around. But Mitch had heard nothing that seemed to actually amount to anything or have a ring of actual truth. Still, it seemed like the entire situation was keeping people on edge, especially the partners.

Mitch had never been one to get in the middle of things. He wasn't outgoing by nature and he didn't deal with conflict well so he never invited it.

Having those personality traits kept him from putting himself out there by asking his brother, Marshall, or either of the other partners anything about it. Besides which, he didn't have a prominent position in the company so none of it really affected him one way or the other. After all, he was just a crew member, although, Manny had been leaving him in charge whenever he got called away more & more often. He wasn't sure what that was about but whatever. He'd step up to help anytime, even though he wasn't getting extra pay for it.

In any event, he figured he was better off to stay out of the fray and let those in charge figure it out. The company heads and the police could do the job. They didn't need him sticking himself in and asking questions. The same was true for what was going on between Manny and Carlos.

Carlos had complained about his lack of hours and he'd given his best input. It was now up to Carlos to act on it. It wasn't his fault if Manny didn't respond the way Carlos wanted. Here again, Mitch was only a crew member and it wasn't his place to confront Manny about the way he'd dismissed Carlos. He was staying out of it, *all of it.*

Mitch watched Carlos slam things around for the next hour before he got in his car and quickly drove away instead of taking lunch break with the rest of the crew like he usually did. Mitch was amazed Manny wasn't picking up on Carlos' mood. He'd left Carlos frustrated by putting him off but didn't even seem to notice his nephew was upset, let alone care. Obviously, Manny had things on his mind. He'd barely spoken to Mitch over the past several days and he really did seem distracted all the time. Mitch supposed it was over this mess with Victor's disappearance but he really didn't know. What he did know was that the Davidson Construction company atmosphere definitely wasn't as good at it once was.

CHAPTER 52

Having looked through Victor's desk Marshall was now armed with the list of notations he's found on the flip calendar. After a good bit of thought he didn't see the point in mentioning anything to Detective Wood until he better understood exactly what he'd discovered. Today he intended to follow up on that and the best place to start was with DeeDee.

DeeDee looked up to see Marshall approaching her with a cup of Dunkin Donuts coffee in hand. She was hoping it was Pumpkin Spice, her favorite flavor. Dunkin Donuts was the only franchise that carried it year round. She wasn't disappointed when Marshall arrived at her desk and handed the cup over.

Marshall valued DeeDee and all she brought to the table each day. He tried to show his appreciation by doing little things like this for her on a regular basis. Today was a little different though. He'd seen how upset she'd been since Victor's disappearance. She was really taking it hard and understandably so. DeeDee's desk was in the center of a hub of offices. One of which was Victors. Marshall had watched them bond easily and quickly when Victor first came on board. Knowing he had left his family behind and would miss them DeeDee had gone the extra distance to help him feel welcomed and cared for. In some ways she'd become a substitute mom to him. In the early days Victor had told her all about his townhouse and she'd helped him with decorating. DeeDee loved thrift shopping and had lent her hand in picking up and refinishing a couple of pieces for him. The two of them conversed quite frequently throughout the course of their work week. She'd been excited with him for his adventurous vacation and was anxious to hear all about it upon his return. Since his disappearance DeeDee had shared with Marshall that Victor had recently mentioned his hopes of meeting a young woman to marry and start a family with. DeeDee was a romantic at heart and was excited to see his plans unfold in the future. Marshall knew she was taking Victor's disappearance as hard as his own family must be. He truly believed DeeDee wanted answers about Victor's whereabouts as much as anyone else.

"So DeeDee," Marshall said to her after she thanked him for the coffee "I wanted to talk with you about something Detective Wood told us the day we met with him. He said it seems you were the last person to see Victor that

145

Thursday before his trip. You mentioned him going into the Vendor File room. Do you happen to know what he was after?"

"Not in detail, no, he was in and out of the room several times. Early in the day he went in and came out with a couple of files. That really wasn't unusual though. He's done that almost all year as part of his follow through on supply orders. He told me when he first started here that he didn't really know how purchasing worked in a construction firm. He was determined to familiarize himself with the process. In an effort to do so he would randomly choose a couple of requisitions each week and follow them through until the checks were cut to pay them. On the ones he was following he'd be the one to attach the check stubs to the original requisition and file them away. That's always the last step in the process. He'd continued doing this because it was helpful for him in understanding the entire process from start to finish. He also considered it part of the checks and balances which is a responsibility he feels the Accounting department should shoulder.

I do know that he'd given himself a deadline on an ongoing project he had set aside a couple of times. He was determined to finish that before taking off on his vacation and was pretty pleased when he finished it at the start of that week. He mentioned in passing one day that something confusing had come up during that process and he hoped to get that cleared up before he left, too."

"Okay, that's interesting and very helpful," Marshall told her before asking, "He didn't give you any more details on what had come up, did he?"

"No," she answered. "But then he wouldn't do that. He took company confidentiality very seriously. I'm sure if he found an actual problem you'd have been his next stop. Generally, I don't pay a lot of attention to what other staff members are doing but I've thought about that afternoon a lot, you know, since he hasn't returned." A shadow of sadness crossed her face as she said that. "And I do remember seeing him bring a file from the Vendor File room out with him to the copier there. He was parked there for quite a while running copies. I think the reason I remember that is that it's not something he had ever done before. I just assumed he'd taken those with him. You might try looking in his brief case. They should be in there for sure, assuming they're not in his desk drawer."

Marshall knew they weren't in the desk. He also knew they weren't in the brief case.

So apparently those were missing now, too.

146

CHAPTER 53

Mason was there to pick up the boys. He hated having to wait in the entry way of his own house as if he weren't the loving husband and father of this home, as if he didn't belong in this house surrounded by his own family. Still, he smiled at Stacey as she approached him.

"I'm so sorry, Mason," she said with an apologetic smile. "Caleb isn't ready yet. He's been dragging his feet all morning. I've sent Declan to hurry him along. They know you're here," she hesitated only a second before she sighed and added, "Oh well, come on into the kitchen and I'll go see how they're coming along."

Hope immediately leapt up in Mason's chest. It was the *first time* she'd invited him anywhere into the house beyond the entryway since their separation. As he followed her into their kitchen he knew he couldn't let this opportunity pass. Thinking fast he answered, "No problem, I'm not in a hurry. In fact, I was running a bit behind myself and kind of rushed out the door. I meant to grab something to drink and forgot so I'm really thirsty. You wouldn't happen to have any of my old favorites in the fridge would you?"

Stacey turned partially toward him and unconsciously flashed that beautiful smile that still made his heart melt. "Actually, I do. What's that they say - 'old habits die hard?' I guess it's true since I find myself still picking it up when I'm at the grocery."

Mason slipped onto one of the counter bar stools as she ducked into the fridge and came out triumphantly holding up a Mountain Dew.

"That's the ticket!" Mason said flashing what he hoped was a winning smile. "Thank you so much!" Then quickly since she'd already taken more than two steps in the direction of the boys' rooms he added "Hey, give the boys a break. Why don't you sit down here and take a minute yourself. It sounds like they've run you ragged today."

She stopped and looked at him hesitantly. They both knew this was an important moment. Was she going to lower the wall between them or keep it firmly erected? Mason could see the struggle in her eyes and secretly wanted to shout for joy when she retraced her steps and reached into the cupboard for a tall glass.

Mason knew what that meant and since she wasn't looking he allowed himself to smile. She was getting herself an iced tea. It was her go-to relaxation drink just as Mountain Dew was his.

Not wanting to miss a beat Mason chatted pleasantly about the boys while she went about filling her glass with ice, retrieving the pitcher from the fridge and pouring the tea over the ice. He had witnessed this ritual thousands of times. Watching her again now may be only a small victory but it was *definitely* a victory!

Not to concede entirely, Stacey said "Let me just go make sure they're still on track before I sit down and enjoy this," Mason nodded and smiled as she headed down the hall to the boys' room. His heart was actually beating a little faster than usual. He *couldn't believe* how much he *still loved this woman.*

It felt *so good* to just be sitting there in the kitchen of the home they'd shared for so many years. His heart literally ached to be living back home with Stacey and his sons. Let it happen, Lord. Please let it happen. Mason surprised himself by praying in his mind. He was also smiling on the inside as he watched Stacey returning.

"They're almost ready," she said as she picked up her iced tea and slid onto the stool beside him. "Actually, you're right," She added turning toward him with a slight chuckle. "They've kept me running all morning. Some day's they just don't seem to be on top of their game, you know? Oh, *I know you do.* We've talked about it so many times, how some days everyone's right on the mark and the day goes so smoothly. Then you've got those days it seems like everyone's out of sorts."

"And today's been one of *those days,*" Mason said meeting her right where she was. It was true. They'd had this conversation many times. It sure felt good slipping back into a familiar place with this woman he'd loved for so long. Within moments they were talking as if they'd never been apart. The topic of conversation moved naturally from the boys to Stacey's job. Before she knew it she was updating Mason on the interactions of the office he'd missed out on while they'd been apart. And time just slipped away. Ten minutes later they were laughing about the incident she'd just shared when they suddenly realized their sons were standing quietly at the entrance to the kitchen looking at them strangely.

The boys hadn't seen their parents interacting much in the past several months. This was the first time their dad had been in the kitchen since the night he'd moved out and there they sat laughing together. They weren't sure what this meant, but it *felt good*.

Mason looked from his sons to his wife's face and immediately realized Stacey was beginning to panic. He couldn't let that happen. Hating to kill the moment but knowing he had to restore the balance Stacey needed right now he quickly stood up from the bar stool, approached the boys and said "Oh, good. You've got your things together! You're ready to roll, right? That's great because we've got places to go and people to see." Turning back to Stacey with a grin, he winked at her while saying, "Thanks so much for the Mountain Dew, Stacey. I was absolutely parched!"

As Stacey took the empty can from his hand her eyes met his and he saw the appreciation in them. Just as he'd hoped would happen the boys had slipped back into their going-with-dad-for-the-weekend mode. *Emotional crisis averted!*

As he'd repeatedly said in this front entrance over the past several months Mason said, "Give your mom a hug, boys, we've got places to be." He stepped aside to let them pass as the boys obediently went into Stacey's waiting arms. Over the tops of their heads her eyes met his and she mouthed the words Thank you, Mason.

With a quick wink he ushered their boys out of the house never doubting that he'd savor that time with Stacey for the rest of the weekend. And that he did!

CHAPTER 54

Marshall made the executive decision to have IT override Victor's password and get him into Victor's computer. He needed to know *exactly* what Victor had been doing in regard to the company's Vendors. Once he was in the system the obvious place to start was the folder on Victors desktop entitled Vendors.

Even though he was now missing, Victor continued to earn Marshall's professional respect. By his documentation, Marshall could see Victor had been frustrated from the start that no complete listing of Vendors the company used for purchasing construction supplies had ever been compiled. He'd put it on his list of things to complete. It was a time consuming process and Victor had gotten derailed a couple of times before becoming diligent in the last month prior to his vacation. He was obviously watching as requisitions came through the Accounting Department and adding each Vendor to his list. According to his final notations he was ninety eight percent sure the list was now complete but intended to go over it more thoroughly upon his return.

Having the list in front of him now Marshall was disappointed there was no vendor listed with two names starting with W. That would've been an easy solution to the WW - ? notation on the flip calendar. Stumped Marshall wasn't sure what to do next.

He spent a bit of time glancing through the rest of the files and documents in Victor's computer. Everything confirmed what an awesome employee and excellent accountant the young man was. But nothing suspicious or odd showed up elsewhere that would lend a reason for his disappearance. Marshall had no choice but to continue pursuing the Vendor information.

Having promised to keep his partners updated on anything he discovered he called a meeting with them and decided to include DeeDee. His thinking was the more heads the more ideas. And it was for that reason that all four of the high back leather chairs in his office were occupied at four o'clock that afternoon.

Marshall shared the steps he'd taken and gave each of them a copy of Victor's completed Vendor List. The four of them then sat staring at it. No one had any ideas off the top of their head.

After a few moments Manny asked DeeDee if she wouldn't mind just relaying to the best of her remembrance her observations and interactions with Victor that Thursday. DeeDee had thought back over that day so many times she felt like she had it completely memorized. The three men sat back and listened intently as DeeDee talked. She described what she had observed as to Victor's trips over to the vendor file room and back to his office. She shared that later he'd gotten one file and spent extended time at the copier apparently running copies of a significant amount of requisitions. Of course, now she wished she'd actually gone over to the copier and spoken with him. Perhaps she'd have glanced at the name of the Vendor Company.

Unfortunately, she hadn't done that. She did remember that she'd offered to make the copies for him and he'd been quite insistent upon doing it himself. Now that she was relaying that it sat a little odd with her. It was as though he actually hadn't wanted her to see. This recollection, of course, peeked all of their interest. It made them feel that perhaps Marshall really was onto something with this Vendor situation.

Marshall, Manny, and Saul felt compassion for DeeDee as she relayed the way she and Victor had talked excitedly together about his pending vacation. It was obvious they'd developed a very close friendship. DeeDee and her husband hadn't been blessed with children in their marriage and there was no question she'd have been a wonderful mother and grandmother. Listening to the way she and Victor interacted they could see that DeeDee felt a motherly love for the young man. DeeDee was getting close to the end of the day in her story when she suddenly stopped talking. The three men sensed her emotional struggle and just sat quietly giving her a moment.

Finally, she lifted her eyes and looked from one to the other her gaze finally resting on Marshall as she said, "I didn't tell this to the police. I haven't said it to anyone before this and it's hard for me to share it even now. But we're all friends here, right?"

Marshall met her gaze dead on as he gently smiled and said, "Absolutely, we are." The other two partners nodded their agreement.

Feeling a little stronger she continued, "Victor had been so happy since his move here. He told me once it was the first brave thing he'd done in his entire life. It had gone so well he was inspired to continue stepping out of his comfort zone. He was beyond excited about his adventures in Ecuador and I couldn't wait to have him return and tell me all about it. He planned to document it all in pictures so we could look through them together. I haven't told any of you this but Victor has become quite special to Gene and me. We've had him over for dinner quite often and he's become almost like family to us. He had such plans for this coming year. He felt secure here with our company and was feeling ready to grow up. That's how he said it. He was ready to grow up and part of that meant to settled down with a wife and eventually have a few children. He'd recently agreed to let me introduce him to the daughter of my only sister once he'd returned from this trip. I know it's silly to think that far ahead but if they'd gotten along he would've actually become my nephew through marriage and would really have been part of my family." There were tears gently falling down her cheeks as she spoke. She wiped them away absentmindedly and said, "This is what I didn't tell the police; just before I left for the day I went into his office to wish him a wonderful trip. I told him he was precious to me and how proud I was of him. Then I gave him a good-bye hug. It was a wonderful moment between us."

She paused briefly before adding, "When I got up the next morning I had a very foreboding feeling. I can't explain it but I felt as if I was never going to see that lovely young man again."

CHAPTER 55

Vonda had just hung up the phone after chatting with Marshall.

She'd grown to look forward to his nightly calls checking that she was safe and secure inside her home. Sometimes it was just a quick check in but other times they chatted a little while, just catching up on each other's lives.

Tonight Marshall had told her about the meeting of the partners and DeeDee. Vonda's heart went out to DeeDee now. She could think of nothing worse than to have someone you know and love come up missing. Not knowing whether they were alive or dead, whether they were in trouble and needing help. Not having any idea where they were, what their mental state was and whether or not they would ever return to be part of your life. Your mind would want to run away with every kind of imagination and worry in such a situation. It would be sheer mental torment!

Vonda simply couldn't imagine having to live with that on a daily basis. She added DeeDee and her husband Gene to her ever growing list of people to pray for. Even right then as she was setting the dishwasher to run she was asking God to be with DeeDee and give her strength and comfort.

Marshall had also shared that he was looking into something Victor was apparently following up on before he went missing. He was hopeful it would lead somewhere to help solve the mystery of what had happened to Victor. Victor's parents had come to town and were now staying in the area. They were checking in with the police frequently in the hopes that their son would be located.

As Vonda proceeded to go about her evening routine she talked with God about everything weighing on her heart. She asked him to be with Victor's parents, DeeDee and Gene, Marshall, the other partners and all of the Davidson Construction family as the police continued investigating Victor's continued absence. She asked God to help them find the truth, whatever that truth was. And that they find Victor. Of course, she prayed that he be found alive and well. She hated to even think it but she also prayed that if some horrendous fate had befallen him God would help that information come out. And give strength and comfort to everyone close to Victor. It was a night of spiritual battle in Vonda's mind. So much was going on and so many people were in need of prayer.

Vonda's faith was such a vital part of her as a person that it was only natural for her to mention God or prayer in her everyday conversations. Still, she realized, not everyone believes in God or the power of prayer. She'd never been one to push her beliefs on others. Being sensitive to spiritual differences she always asked instead of assuming it was alright if she prayed for someone when they'd shared that they were struggling. Many times people would smile, thank her and tell her that would be wonderful.

There had also been occasions where people were confused by the very concept. They told her no. She didn't need to do that as they didn't believe in or need prayer. If someone was interested she'd gladly share her faith but Vonda never pushed or argued over spiritual beliefs. She did however, have a sense of sadness for those who didn't believe. Vonda couldn't imagine her life without her faith in God and the power of prayer. It was such a source of comfort, strength and peace in her journey through life. But more than that she'd seen with her own eyes and felt in her own being the presence of God and His power. She had felt His love for her in a very personal way on so many occasions. She could specifically share those moments in which there was no other explanation but that God had intervened, comforted, brought peace or met the need of the moment in a supernatural way. Vonda's life was a virtual demonstration of the quote by Stuart Chase "For those who believe no proof is necessary. For those who don't believe no proof is possible."

Having completed her nightly tasks and gotten ready for bed, Vonda went to her bedroom and settled in. She thought about reading for a while but decided against it. She was so emotionally and spiritually tired that as her dear Stanley used to tell her he'd witnessed many times she was literally asleep before her head had even hit the pillow.

CHAPTER 56

Unsure of what else to do Marshall decided to go through the Vendor files starting with the W Vendors. Truthfully, he had no idea what the notation WW - ? on Victors flip calendar meant. But DeeDee was certain Victor had been copying requisitions from a Vendor file on his last day at work so this seemed as good a place as any to start.

He had DeeDee cancel all of his morning appointments and went to the Vendor file room. After telling DeeDee what he planned she went in with him and pulled the first W Vendor file out. She opened the file and proceeded to explain the layout of the paperwork inside. She first noted that the document attached inside the left side of the file was the service contract for the company. Each of those was signed by Marshall himself.

Years ago Marshall had set a policy that no company could become a Vendor without submitting an application which he himself would peruse and approve or disapprove. Once they became a Vendor the contract had to be renewed every five years. Obviously, Marshall was aware of this policy. He was also very familiar with Vendor Service Contracts. The rest of the file was filled with requisitions for supplies. Those were routinely submitted when supplies were ordered. Once the supplies were received the date was noted on the requisition and it was submitted to accounting for payment. When the checks arrived the check stubs were attached to the requisition and it was stamped PAID. The actual check was mailed or delivered to the Vendor. At that point the completed requisition was placed into the file in the Vendor file room.

DeeDee offered to go through the files with Marshall. Being as he really wasn't sure exactly what he was looking for he thanked her but declined. He might go through the entire W section and find nothing. If that happened he would feel better knowing that he himself had looked through each and every file and found nothing amiss. Besides which it was difficult to accept DeeDee's help when he couldn't tell her exactly what to look for. After DeeDee left him alone he began his search.

As the morning passed it was driven home to Marshall exactly how much his company had grown. He remembered when he first started out. There were only two vendors he routinely used to purchase building supplies. Taking a brief break he placed his hands mid-back and leaned backward. As he stretched he looked around at all the file cabinets in the room. It was actually amazing to think his company had gone from only two Vendors then to an entire room of Vendor files now.

Marshall took a moment to just be thankful. He truly felt blessed.

An hour later DeeDee showed up with a cup of coffee. He thanked her and stayed with it. Although Marshall didn't order supplies these days he did recognize the majority of the Vendors by name as he was going through the files. Occasionally, though, he came across a file where the company name didn't ring a bell. He'd been glancing at a few requisitions in each file all along but he paid a bit more attention when he came to an unfamiliar Vendor. If for no other reason than to see what type of supplies they were providing. He was also taking notice of which of his construction crew members signed the requisitions to order the supplies.

After a solid two hours he was considering taking a break when he pulled out the next file. The name on the vendor was Wentworth. Marshall wasn't at all familiar with a company called Wentworth.

As with each file up to this point he opened the file and his eyes immediately sought his own signature at the bottom of the Service Contract attached immediately to the left hand side. It wasn't there. In fact he didn't even see a signature or date line at the bottom of the page. Looking more closely he realized the service contract pages had been clipped into the file in the wrong order. He lifted the first page and saw that the sheet had been inverted. The signature was actually on the back side of the front page. It was a simple error made during filing. It was easily corrected. Marshall proceeded to disengage the bar holding the papers in place across the top of file. Removing the pages he flipped them around and quickly placed them in the correct order. Finding the signature page he glanced down to confirm his signature and clip the pages back into the file. When he saw his signature something didn't seem right.

Marshall lifted the page to take a closer look at his signature. It was amazingly similar but it wasn't actually his signature. Even as he had that thought he couldn't imagine being correct. Who would forge his signature to a service contract and why? Wait. What had he just asked himself? Was he actually thinking someone had forged his signature? He lifted the page and again studied it very closely. He had not signed this document. But if he hadn't, who had?

He put the service contract pages together and laid them on the left hand side of the file before turning to look at the rest of the file. As with each of the proceeding files it was full of requisitions. He picked the top one up and began to look it over. He read through the vendor information at the top of the form. Wentworth Construction Supply Company it said. That was followed by an address, phone number and email address. Everything seemed in order. He then looked at the supplies listed. Nothing unusual stood out there. At the bottom of the page was the date and signature of the crew member placing the order. Again, nothing seemed amiss, onto the next requisition. Marshall was five requisitions in when it dawned on him that every requisition in this file so far had been signed by the exact same employee. That seemed odd. A few minutes later after Marshall had looked at every requisition in the Wentworth file he stood thinking.

First of all, the service contract was forged and secondly every requisition was signed by the same person. Staring at the contact information at the top of the requisition Marshall found himself wondering if the company was even real. Suddenly he said to himself very softly, "WW?" Did Victor separate the vendor name when he made the notation? Could WW actually stand for Wentworth?

CHAPTER 57

Mason woke up in a cold sweat. The bed sheets were drenched and his heart was pounding. He'd been back there again. *Why, oh why, couldn't he just put it all behind him?* Why did it have to keep pulling him back there in his dreams making him see it happening all over again.

It wasn't like this in the beginning. He'd done what he had to do and moved on. He was doing so well living his daily life and getting past it. Right up until he started going to counseling.

The dreams started after he began seeing Dr. Rossman. Actually they started shortly after he first attended Grief Share. They didn't seem like dreams when they were happening though. It seemed as if he was right there reliving the worst night of his life all over again. He didn't know how much longer he could take this. *How was he supposed to live like this?*

Things were going so much better between him and Stacey now. He was beginning to have hope she would soon ask him to come back home. But how could he do that with this going on? He couldn't be having these nightmares and waking up in a sweat with her beside him. She'd want to know what was troubling him. *He had to get over this.* He had to make this stop before he could go home again. What was he going to do?

He kept thinking about telling Dr. Rossman what he'd done. But he knew if he did they would have to go to the police.

Sure, she was bound by doctor/patient confidentiality but she was sure to encourage him to turn himself in. There was *no doubt* she was going to expect him to do the right thing. He couldn't confess to her unless he was prepared to confess to everyone. Every fiber of his being was against that. He couldn't take the humiliation of having the entire world know who he really was inside. What he was really capable of. And once Stacey knew what he'd done it would ruin everything. How could he expect her to take him back after that?

He rolled over in his bed and moaned loudly. He sounded as if his soul was in anguish. *Well, it was.* He was tormented by what he'd done and tormented by what he might have to do to get over it.

Dr. Rossman had told him the road to mental health wasn't easy. In fact, she'd said it could be downright brutal. He'd had no idea *this* was what she meant. This was definitely brutal. He wanted to be healthy though. He wanted to be freed of all his demons. But he didn't want to lose *everything he loved* in the process.

He lay there struggling with his thoughts until his mind and spirit could take no more. Finally, he fell back into a restless sleep.

Waking up three hours later when the alarm went off Mason rolled out of bed and stumbled into the shower. He was rested enough to function but not enough to shake the images of the nightmares completely from his brain. It was going to be a long day. He had an appointment with Dr. Rossman that evening and he *wasn't at all sure* what he was going to do about that.

He was seriously wrestling with what he should and shouldn't tell her. He did trust her a great deal. He knew she was there to help him on a professional level. He also believed she cared deeply about him on a personal level, if that made sense. They weren't involved in each other's personal lives. They didn't socialize or have a personal relationship. That wasn't what he meant. But he had told her so much about himself. And she took a genuine interest in all of it. She wanted him to achieve good mental health and have the happy life with Stacey and the boys he not only wanted, but needed. That was what he meant. Dr. Rossman cared about his personal life and wanted the best for him. Maybe if he told her what was holding him back she really could help him figure out what to do and how to deal with it so it no longer stood in the way.

Maybe he *would* tell her everything.

Dressed for the work day he ate his breakfast, packed his lunch and headed to the Hardee Street projects. For the first time in his life he loved what he was doing. He was finally in a good place and everything was going well. Everything but not being home with Stacey and the boys. He knew the counseling and Grief Share were helping him peel back the layers he'd needed to peel back for years. He could see healing and happiness on the horizon but for this one thing that tormented him.

He just had to find a way to rid himself of that *one terrible night*.

CHAPTER 58

Marshall was heartsick as he put the Wentworth file away. He'd seen enough to know this had to be what Victor had stumbled upon. What it meant as to his disappearance remained to be seen but Marshall now knew he and his company had been betrayed.

The Wentworth Company wasn't real.

It didn't exist. It had been conjured up, falsely created. A Vendor application was never submitted. His signature on the vendor contract was a forgery. Once the file was created and successfully placed into the Vendor file room the rest was easy. It was just a matter of submitting falsified requisitions for imaginary supplies. Given the company's fast pace of growth more and more vendors had begun to be utilized. The accountant at the time had been close to retirement. It must've been easy to slip a bogus company into the mix and begin cashing the checks.

Marshall had been duped.

Davidson Construction Company was the victim of embezzlement and had been for over three years. What that meant in actual dollars Marshall hadn't taken the time to calculate. He was too disgusted, angered, disappointed and shocked to take anything else in at the moment.

He was shell shocked. He felt physically ill. Sick to his stomach and in a haze. How could someone close to him, someone he cared for and trusted do this to him?

He wasn't ready to reveal what he'd discovered to DeeDee or anyone else just yet. So he plastered on the most natural smile as he could manage and left the file room.

Looking up from her desk DeeDee asked, "Any luck?"

Keeping the smile in place he side stepped by answering, "Wow, time got away from me in there. I'm famished. I'm gonna duck out and grab some lunch. You should probably do the same soon. I'll catch up with you after I've eaten."

She turned back to her work with a quick, "I'm right behind you as soon as I finish this up."

Marshall knew he had to go to the police. There was no way around it. He just wasn't sure he shouldn't try dealing with this himself first. Should he tell the partners? Should he just go confront the issue himself? Was that what Victor had done? If so, what had happened then?

He was still trying to actually absorb what he'd seen. There had to be some mistake. There was no way this was really happening, was there? It's not possible. It's simply not possible that this is real. His mind began to repeat over and over as he walked to his car. Sitting behind the wheel Marshall was overcome. He leaned his forehead down onto the steering wheel. What was he going to do now?

Finally, he put the car in gear and drove away. He actually was famished so he decided to get lunch. He was tempted to talk with someone but he knew once he did that he'd have to actually do something about what he'd learned. He, along with everyone else in the company, was feeling the stress of having an employee gone missing. After what he had just learned he was in shock. He was also hungry. The best thing he could do right now was to be alone and eat something. He decided to go to an out of the way little hamburger joint he liked.

He could almost guarantee he wouldn't run into anyone he knew there and he really needed this time to think. There was a lot to try to put together. He wasn't completely sure yet but, sadly, he was beginning to suspect he might actually know where Victor was.

CHAPTER 59

This was the second therapy session Stacey was attending with Mason and Dr. Rossman.

In the first session Mason had shared all he had recently been learning about himself and what he was accomplishing through counseling. That session had gone so well that the two of them had started spending more time together. Stacey felt they were reconnecting after living in a tense and estranged relationship which was mostly due to Mason's out of control anger. As the weeks passed since the first session she had attended she'd felt herself falling more deeply in love with her husband.

Mason, in turn, had a renewed hope of returning home to his wife and a healed relationship with her. He had always loved Stacey deeply. He now realized that because of his damaged spirit he'd been unable to truly show her that.

In one of his past sessions with Dr. Rossman Mason had become quite emotional. He ended the session telling her something terrible had happened which he'd never told anyone about and had no intention of telling her. It was a heart wrenching session for both of them. In the weeks that followed Dr. Rossman had worked tirelessly to completely win Mason's trust. Once he trusted her he was able to open that wound and share the ugly truth with her. Today he was going to share it with Stacey.

This would be one of the hardest things Mason had ever done.

After Dr. Rossman greeted the two of them she turned the session over to Mason.

Mason turned to his wife and took her hands in his. He spent a few minutes telling her how precious the past month since their last session together had been to him. He told her in no uncertain terms how deeply he loved her. How thankful that she'd waited over twenty years for them to finally have the kind of connection he knew she had always wanted. He talked about the importance of communication in marriage, the importance of truth and honesty. Then he took a deep breath and told her he hadn't been completely honest with her. Today he was going to remedy that.

Stacey felt a catch in her heart. What was her husband about to tell her? And would she be able to forgive him and still love him after hearing it?

Mason took a deep breath and looked at Dr. Rossman. She smiled slightly and nodded for him to continue.

"Stacey, this isn't going to be easy for me to say or for you to hear. The only thing I ask is that you hear me out. If you can keep from interrupting, asking questions or reacting until I've told you everything it'll go easier, for both of us, I think. Try not to speculate. Just listen and let me tell you what I have to tell you in my own way. When I'm done I'll answer anything you want to ask me.

I hope you can talk to me right away but if you need time to process and decide if you can try to trust me again I'll give you all the time you need. Just know, no matter what's happened, no matter what I've done, that *I've never stopped loving you.*"

Stacey needed to avoid looking at him so she looked down at her lap. Her heart was in her throat. *What was he telling her?* Had he cheated on her? That was the worse betrayal she could think of. She would never have imagined that Mason would cheat on her. Is that what he was saying? But wait, he'd asked her not to speculate. To just listen and let him tell her what he needed to. She'd do that. Yes, she *could do that.* She took a deep breath to steel herself against what she was about to hear. She lifted her head, looked her husband in the eyes and told him to continue.

"I lied to you, Stace. I'm so sorry. I didn't know what else to do at the time. I did something terrible and I couldn't let you find out. So I lied. As you know I've had a lot of jobs through the years. I've had such a hard time keeping a job. Well, this was when I was working that job that kept me on the road so much. You remember. It wasn't that long ago. It was the last job I had before I finally asked Marshall to take me on as a crew member. You remember that time I called you from Atlanta and told you the job had been extended? I wasn't sure how long I'd have to stay but I couldn't come home yet. I called a couple of more times. I ended up being gone just short of 3 months. It was the longest I'd ever been away without at least coming home on a weekend to see you. I know you remember this."

She nodded that she remembered. It had been a very hard time for her.

"Well, most of that was a lie. I'm so sorry, Stace. I hope you can forgive me. It was all just stupid, crazy, really. But I couldn't tell you what I'd done.

CHAPTER 60

Stacey's heart was pounding. She was as tense as she thought she'd ever been. She sat waiting to hear the next words her husband was going to say. She hoped and prayed that she could forgive him once she knew whatever it was that he'd done.

Mason could see the anxiety in her eyes and knew there was only one way to get passed it. He had to keep going. He had to do this. *He had to tell her everything.* He had to let the chips fall where they may. Just wanting this over with he took a deep breath and went on, "that was a nasty job. It was grunt work, just dirty, filthy, manual labor all day long. When I got off work I just wanted to relax. I was drinking way too much and being away from you made that easier. I got in a bad habit of going to this dive bar not far from where I was staying. The drinks were cheap and the people were just bad seed. So this one night, I don't know maybe only the third week into that job I was at the bar again. I got pretty drunk and was acting stupid. I stayed there drinking way into the morning hours. There was this guy there who took issue with me. He was a big guy and I knew it'd be stupid to try and fight him. But he just kept eggin' me on. It was almost like he was trying to pick a fight. We got into it a couple of times but another man in the bar pulled us off each other. Anyway, he finally left. About a half an hour went by and I'd had enough so I stumbled out of there and headed back to my hotel. I wouldn't risk a DUI so I was walking to this bar every time I went. So this night, too, I was on foot.

Well, this guy had laid in wait for me to leave. I was only, I don't know, maybe five hundred feet from the bar when he stepped out of the shadows in an alley I'd cut through. He must've seen me coming and ducked in there.

He started in on me again, just saying stupid stuff. I told him to get away and leave me be. I wasn't interested in fighting him. And I really wasn't. But you know me, Stace, I can get mad and drinking only adds to it. I was already on a short fuse that night and he was just stepping along right beside me poking at me and makin' digs. I was holding off pretty good until he started in calling me a 'momma's boy'. He must've seen a reaction in my eyes because he latched on like a dog on bone. I told him to stop. *I did!* I said 'leave my mother out of this.' Oh, he laughed at that. He doubled over. For whatever reason, he was having fun. Then he just went to it. He kept making digs about my mom. Finally, I told him 'she's dead, man. You're talkin' trash about a dead woman.' That just added fuel to his flame. It was really upsetting me. Finally, he grabbed me by the shoulders. He looked me in the face and what he said next was just the worst! It was unforgiveable! I lost it! I mean I can't even tell you - it felt like all the anger I'd been carrying around inside me for twenty years just exploded outta me. I turned loose on that man. I mean, it didn't matter that I was drunk. It didn't matter that he was bigger and stronger than me. All that mattered was that I was mad and he was there. I wailed on him. I knocked him down. I smashed into his face. I stood up and kicked him in his ribs. *I showed no mercy.*

Finally, I leaned over and grabbed him by the throat and squeezed. I wanted to squeeze the life right outta him. To me he was as good as dead. So there I was lookin' into that ugly, smashed up, bloody face. I was lookin at his eyes when slowly I started to see the life going from his eyes. Somehow, I realized what I was doing. It started to register in my head what I was doing. I let him go and his head fell to the ground. He was lifeless. I looked around in a frenzy. There was no one in that alley. *No one had seen.* I jumped up and ran. I ran to my hotel as fast as I could in my drunken state. I washed the blood from my face and hands. My hands were a mess from the beating I'd given him.

I had nothing but Vaseline in my hotel room so I spread that all over the wounds on my hands just before I fell into bed. I pretty much passed out and then I just slept it off.

When I woke up the next morning the whole night was a blur. Just shaded scenes all mixed up in my mind. But I remembered some of that fight in the alley and my hands proved it had happened. I didn't know what to do. I mean, I'd killed a man, hadn't I? I wasn't even sure what had happened. So I waited 'til way late in the day, just before dark, then I took a cab to another area of town. I went to a drug store. I got a pair of gloves and put 'em on right there. I gathered some medical supplies to treat my hands with, but they were messed up bad. I bought it all and went back to my hotel.

I called you that day and lied to you for the first time in our married life. I mean a big lie, Stace. I told you the company had more work for me and had asked me to stay on. I didn't know how long. The truth? I never went back there. I spent the next week hold up in my room nursing my wounds. I

165

watched the news trying to find out about that man I'd beat up. Did he live or did he die?

Finally, I saw a write up about a man who'd been found beaten badly, almost dead in an alley. He'd been taken to the hospital and was in ICU. It looked like he was gonna make it but the police were trying to piece together what happened to him. They were lookin' for a person of interest in the beating that took place.

I left that night after dark. I drove 100 miles west and got another dive hotel room. I stayed there the next 5 weeks until my hands had healed. I was lying every time I called you. I didn't get paid in all that time. I lied about that, too. *I'm so sorry Stacey*." A sob caught in his throat. It took a minute before he could go on. "I pulled money out of Declan's college fund to pay the bills for over 3 months. I'm so sorry, Stacey. *I'm so sorry*, babe. I know we didn't have much in there to start with but I've put it all back now that I'm working for Marshall. I covered *it all*, babe.

I've been so ashamed of what my anger led me to. I was *never* gonna tell you *any of this*. I was never telling *anyone* about any of this. But it's been tearing me up. Oh, it's been killing me all this time. I mean, I saw who I really was that night and I never wanted you to know what I'm capable of.

Then that day you drew back from me the way you did it all came flooding back. I saw myself beating that man ruthlessly. I don't even know how that happened!! I didn't know I was capable of that kind of rage. But I looked in your eyes and I saw pure fear and *I knew* it was justified. Even though, I truly believe I'd never hurt you. I knew you were right when you told me to leave and it's been killing me, Stace. You *saw it in me*. Somehow, you *knew me* better than I knew myself. You were right to make me leave and I knew it. *That's why* I found Dr. Rossman. I knew if I didn't find out why that happened, if I didn't find a way to deal with all that anger...I mean, if it could happen once, it could happen again. Maybe it could happen with someone I knew and even loved. Maybe even you or one of our boys. Oh, God forbid it but maybe that was possible." He was crying out right now, with sobs that rose up from deep inside him. Finally, in a broken voice he said "Oh, God Stacey, I'll live *the rest of my life alone* before I'll *ever* let that happen. I'll *never* hurt you or our boys. I love you all *so much*!"

Huge tears were streaming down his face, Stacey's, too. She took him into her arms as she gently said, "Shhhh, you shush now Mason. It's okay. It's all

166

gonna be okay, now," she raised her face until her eyes met those of Dr. Rossman. Stacey's eyes were asking *what can I do? How can I help this man I love?*

Dr. Rossman smiled and said, "Yes, it is. You're right Stacey. It's all going to be okay now. You two can work through this now."

These were the moments Dr. Rossman lived for. *This was healing in its purest form.*

CHAPTER 61

Marshall was seated at his desk when Mitch knocked lightly on the door frame. Marshall looked up and smiled.

"Hey Mitch, come on in and have a seat," he said continuing to grin. "I haven't seen you around lately and thought it'd be good to catch up a bit."

"Yeah?" Mitch said. Looking a little confused as he moved into the office and sat down in the leather chair opposite Marshall's desk. "Not much going on with me these days. Same ol' same ol', ya know? What about you?"

"Well, there's been a lot going on, actually," Marshall said. "You know about Victor's disappearance, I'm sure."

"Yeah, yeah. Heard about that. Strange, huh?"

"Very strange," Marshall agreed, looking as sad as he felt. Making eye contact with his younger brother he added, "Some other strange things have been going on as well, it seems."

Mitch looked a little uncomfortable and took a quick look around the room as if to make sure they were the only two there before he answered, "Really? I'm not sure what you're referring to there."

"Oh, you're not?" Marshall said as he dropped the Wentworth file onto the desk right between them. "Maybe this will help," nodding toward the file.

Mitch's head tilted toward the desk as his eyes took in the name on the file. The color began to drain out of his face but he didn't say a word.

Marshall waited.

After a full minute had passed Marshall said simply, "I have no idea how you could do this to me, Mitch."

Without hesitation Mitch responded, "Really? *Really Marshall?* You have *no idea* how *I* could do this *to you*? Well, do you have any idea how *you could do this to me*, then? That's what I want to know. I mean I've worked for you *for years* and not once did you *ever think* to include me in this business empire you've created. Your two *tree-house building boyhood friends* are good enough to *profit nicely* from your success - *but not Mitch*! No sirree, not your *own, dear, brother*! I mean really! What does a man have to do before he's good enough for you?"

Marshall was astonished at the anger spewing from Mitch. He'd had *no idea* Mitch felt this way. Marshall was speechless. It didn't matter because Mitch wasn't done. "All my life I've taken a back seat. First to Mason, oh, you look surprised. Yes, that's right. I took a back seat to Mason *every day of my life*. He was mom's *precious baby boy,"* he said with great distain, "but it got even worse after you took us in. You were too busy dealing with all his fights and shenanigans to even think about me. You were working at your precious construction company day and night but you sure made time for Mason, didn't you?

Oh, don't look so shook up," he said condescendingly. "It wouldn't have mattered if you hadn't cost me the only person I've *ever* loved. When mom and dad died *I didn't need you!* In fact, *I've NEVER needed you!!!*

I didn't need you then because I had Peggy. Oh, you didn't know about her, did you? Yeah, that's right. Peggy Wentworth. That was her name and *I loved her!!!* She was my girl. *I loved her,* Marshall, but you? YOU *took her away from me.* She's the only one I've ever loved and I lost her *because of you!*"

Marshall had no idea what Mitch was talking about. He didn't remember anyone by that name. He didn't remember Mitch dating anyone or even talking about a girl at all back then. How could he have missed something so huge?

Mitch was crying now. He was spewing the angry words at Marshall but at the same time he was crying. His emotions were totally out of control.

He sat there trying to get a handle on his emotions. Finally, he started to calm down.

"She didn't leave me right away," he said in a calmer voice. "Not while I could still see her at school. But it wasn't like before when we were seeing each other on Sundays and Wednesday and half the time on Saturdays. Now it was just at school and that *just wasn't enough.* It wasn't enough for her but it was *all I could manage* so she hung on. But then school let out for the summer. See, I already couldn't get to church to see her. We lived too far away and you weren't there to take us. Even when you were there *you weren't there.* You weren't asking me what I wanted, what I needed. Nah, you thought you had it all figured out. All we needed was for you to get legal custody. Beyond that you just didn't care. You didn't care that I needed to get to church to see my girl. So that was the beginning of the end. Once school was out it wasn't long 'til she got tired of waiting to see me. And that's when Bentley Gates moved in. She's married to Bentley now. *Do you know that, Marshall?* She didn't love him. *She loved ME!!* But you took me away from her. Yeah, it's all your fault. *Don't you see?*"

169

Marshall couldn't believe this. He wasn't sitting across from his forty two year old brother anymore. He'd reverted back to a seventeen year old boy with a broken heart. That was what was at the heart of the matter? Losing his first love? That was why he'd done all of this? *It was beyond comprehension.*

"I figured you owed me after all that," Mitch said. He was calm now. "I didn't know how or when but I knew someday I was gonna make you pay. I thought about it for years. I thought long and hard, you see? It was always about the business for you and things just kept getting better and better. Here you are raking the money in. So I figured the best place to hurt you was in the wallet. And hey, I can always use the extra bucks." He laughed at that point.

It was an ugly hate-filled laugh.

"And you were only too happy to have me join the crew weren't you, big brother? Good ol' Marshall always there to bail his little brothers out. Take 'em in when life deals 'em a bad blow. And here I am, *ten yeeeaaaarrs later*" He dragged the word out to make his point, still workin' the construction crew. You ever think I might want more than this, Marshall? You ever think about offering your little brother a leg up in your company? *Nah, guess not.*"

Marshall was still in shock but he was starting to recover. He had no idea how to respond to all of this. Was there any point in defending himself? He'd had no idea young Mitch had a girl at church he wanted to see. He had no memory of Mitch ever trying to talk to him about that, never even asking about a ride anywhere. Marshall had just thought Mitch was content with the way things were going and hadn't wanted to be a bother. He had actually appreciated Mitch being easy since Mason had been so difficult. He'd been *totally blind* to everything Mitch had just said.

How ironic that the partners had just discussed offering Mitch the newly created position for a third crew leader. Manny had purposely been leaving Mitch in charge to gage how he would handle the extra responsibility. They'd all been very pleased. Choosing not to defend himself Marshall decided to just get to the matter at hand.

Where's Victor, Mitch?" He asked simply.

A shadow crossed Mitch's face. Marshall thought he actually caught a glimpse of something deep and real, Sadness? Remorse? He wasn't sure what it was.

CHAPTER 62

Where's Victor?" Marshall repeated.

Mitch didn't answer.

It seemed the wind had left his sails. Gone was the anger, the sarcasm, the hatred. He looked defeated.

"Yeah, that wasn't supposed to happen," he finally said quietly without looking up.

Marshall felt relief flood through his body. Mitch wasn't going to deny it. He wasn't going to fight this.

"I figured as much," Marshall said before adding, "He figured it out, didn't he?"

Mitch still wasn't looking up.

"Yeah, yeah, he did," nodding his head yes. "He didn't know he did, really. But he did. He showed up that night with the requisitions asking if the company was real."

Finally, Mitch lifted his head and looked his older brother in the eyes.

"I mean, come on. He *knew* it wasn't," Mitch said simply.

"What happened?" Marshall asked gently, realizing his forty two year old brother had now returned.

"It was an accident," Mitch said simply. "*It really was*, Marshall. *You gotta believe me*. I'd never hurt anyone on purpose. And I'd never *do that* to anyone.

We were arguing. He raised his hand holding those requisitions over his head and demanding to know if the company was real. I lunged at him. I just wanted the requisitions. I wanted to make 'em go away. I just wanted to tear 'em to shreds and never have to think about 'em again. He took a step back and lost his footing. He went down. I didn't see it but he must've smacked his head on the Island, the new island in the kitchen. I heard the crack, you know, when his head hit. I just didn't realize it until later.

Looked like he was gone by the time he hit the floor but I didn't know. I was so caught up in my own anger. I was screaming at him. It took a minute to realize he wasn't getting up, wasn't responding at all. Isn't that just my luck - to kill a man without meaning to?"

He lifted his hands and put his face into them as soft sobs shook his shoulders.

Marshall got up from his desk and walked around it. He gently took his brother into his arms and held him as he cried. Mitch leaned into Marshall's shoulder.

"I'm sorry Marshall," he sobbed. "I *am so sorry!!*"

Marshall just held him until he'd calmed down and stopped sobbing.

"He's in the driveway, isn't he, Mitch?" Marshall asked calmly.

Marshall had deduced it all from Lilly's reaction to Mitch. When that happened Marshall knew Mitch had abducted and returned Vonda. He just didn't understand why.

After Vonda told Marshall what she'd seen and heard and that the driveway was poured the next day he'd checked the dates and noted that the driveway was poured the Friday Victor's vacation started. Once he knew Mitch had been embezzling from the company everything had fallen into place.

Finally, Mitch raised his head. When their eyes met Marshall knew the answer to his question. Victor *was* buried in the driveway.

Mitch suppressed a sob as he said again, "I'm sorry, Marshall. I'm so sorry for *everything.*"

Marshall was sorry, too, especially when Detective Andrew Wood and his two officers stepped out of the large office closet and approached them.

When Marshall had taken the Wentworth file to Detective Wood they'd come up with the plan for Marshall to confront Mitch, giving him a chance to come clean. Marshall chose the location and time of the meeting. He wanted it at the end of the work day so it would be well past working hours when the meeting ended.

It was his way of ensuring none of the staff would be there to see his brother taken away in handcuffs.

CHAPTER 63

Vonda stretched and rolled over as her mind and body told her it was time to come to life for the day. By the time her feet hit the floor she'd already thanked God for another day of precious life and was praying for her family and friends. She opened the bedroom blinds and let the beautiful sunshine flood into the room before gathering her clothing and heading for the shower.

A short time later after petting Lilly and filling her food dish Vonda picked up her steaming coffee mug and headed for the sliders. Stepping out onto the patio she settled into her rocking chair. She glanced over at Ivy and Dan's house as she thought about the happenings on Hardee Street.

They'd handled things as well as any new home owner could, she supposed. Being told a man was buried under your driveway and his body must be recovered wasn't news you'd hear every day. Thankfully, it wasn't news most people would hear in a lifetime.

Of course, Davidson Construction had covered the costs. Once the repairs were done there was nothing to indicate their property had ever been disturbed. No one who didn't already know the story would ever be the wiser. But then, most everyone knew the story. It had been a headliner in their small town newspaper and across the state.

The autopsy evidence supported Mitch's story. Victor's death was ruled accidental. Mitch was charged with abuse of a corpse. He pled guilty so there was no need for a lengthy trial. His attorney told him to expect to spend a minimum of one year behind bars. To his thinking one year wasn't nearly enough in repayment of Victor's life. His attorney explained that since the death itself was unintentional and accidental the sentence wasn't for Victor's life. It was for the crime of covering it up and burying his body.

His brother and the partners decided not to press charges for Mitch's embezzlement from the company. Mitch was filled with remorse and insistent on paying back what he'd taken. To that end he immediately sold his house and turned the money over to the company. Charges were instated by the police along with charges for Vonda's abduction. Mitch entered a guilty plea in both cases.

While in jail awaiting sentencing Mitch wrote letters of remorse to the Davidson Construction company partners, Vonda and Victor's family. His attorney submitted copies to the judge. With this being Mitch's first legal offense, the partial return of the money from his house sale and the letters of remorse his attorney was hopeful for a lenient sentence, perhaps community service instead of added jail time.

Mitch would willingly accept whatever punishment the judge deemed fair.

Upon Mason's recommendation Mitch agreed to pursue counseling. Dr. Rossman agreed to have sessions at the jail while he awaited sentencing and following his conviction.

Mitch felt terrible for the anguish his actions had caused Victor's family and friends. He *couldn't believe* what he'd done and who he'd allowed himself to become.

In Vonda's letter he gave a heartfelt apology for what he'd put her through. He then admitted her prayers had not only unnerved him they'd been instrumental in changing his course of action. Vonda could do nothing but *thank God* for His protection and guidance through the whole ordeal.

Mitch admitted in therapy and privately to Marshall that another motivation in taking the money had been his attempt to impress Lucille, who was used to a more extravagant lifestyle. Lucille, however, cut him out of her life *the moment* she learned of his arrest.

Dr. Rossman told Mitch self-forgiveness is often the hardest forgiveness to obtain. They'd be pursuing that topic in their future sessions. Mitch didn't doubt it one bit. He *was amazed* at the forgiveness and grace being extended to him by those he'd so grievously wronged. *He felt most undeserving!*

He honestly wasn't sure what he thought about God or faith but he was extremely grateful for Vonda's prayers. He felt blessed for the way everyone was treating him in the face of all he'd done. If this was an example of God's grace he *couldn't deny being drawn to it.*

Carlos eventually did get to speak with Manny about his frustrations and the partners all agreed to bring him on full-time. The other long-term crew members were considered and the new crew leader position, which Mitch had been in line for, was filled to everyone's satisfaction. There was no denying the whole situation had impacted Marshall's company but everyone was moving forward.

Mason and Stacey reconciled and the boys were thrilled to have their dad move back home. The couple began to share openly that their marriage had become stronger than ever before. Mason shared his renewed faith with

Stacey and his sons and they excitedly began a new spiritual quest as a family.

With Stacey's help Mason was able to locate the man he had injured. His name was Aaron Michaels. He agreed to meet with Mason who asked his forgiveness and offered to repay his medical costs. Stating he was willing to accept the legal consequences of his actions he also offered to turn himself in to the police. Aaron admitted that his actions had greatly contributed to the situation and said that wasn't necessary. He shared with Mason that the whole incident was a wake-up call in his life and he had since made significant changes. The two men found they had much in common and have chosen to stay in touch. They are currently on the pathway to a lifelong friendship, it would seem. Further proof that God works in ways we just cannot imagine.

Rocking gently as the sun warmed her face and the gentle breeze played with loose strands of her hair Vonda sat thinking over everything that happened. She could so clearly see God at work in all of their lives. Without knowing what all was happening behind the scenes, she'd begun praying for the construction crew, adding Marshall and his brothers early in their friendship. How many times had she prayed for Mitch as she'd seen him coming and going? It was a tragic situation to be sure. But through it all there was *no denying* the power of prayer!

Looking across the back yard at the completed homes on Hardee Street Vonda's thoughts went to her beloved Stanley. He'd be even more pleased with the neighborhood they'd chosen if he could see it now.

When they purchased their house the realtor explained that all of Hardee Street would one day have new homes on it. They were to expect construction over the next several years. Stanley had laughed and commented he wasn't one to complain about construction noise. This was probably some kind of payback for all the times he'd disturbed his neighbors while building sheds or updating their past homes. They'd all had a good chuckle over that.

Oh, Stanley, Vonda thought fondly, what a tale I could tell you now. She smiled at the thought.

Knowing Stanley, there was no doubt he'd be happy Vonda had found a protective and kind friend in Marshall. And for all the new friends she'd met through him, the ball players and their families. Mason, Stacey, Declan and Caleb. The love in that family warmed her heart every time she was with them, which was pretty often as she now attended many of the boys' sports and school events. She and Stacey had quickly become good friends. Vonda had joined Stacey's monthly book club and Stacey was now attending the women's Bible study on Wednesday evenings with Vonda.

And Vonda's circle of friends continued to grow.

Once the discovery of Victor's death became public knowledge Vonda had reached out to DeeDee. Being acquainted with grief herself she wanted to be there for DeeDee in her grief over the loss of Victor. The two women had since become quite close. Being near the same age they found they had many common experiences and interests.

Still relaxing on her back patio Vonda reflected on her friendship with Marshall. What a blessing! Marshall had sat on this very patio with her when he'd taken on the terrible task of telling her it was his own brother, Mitch, who had abducted her and why. Marshall said he didn't want to minimize the power of prayer but he held firm to the fact that Mitch had *never been a murderer*. He firmly believed Mitch would have returned her unharmed regardless. He was also certain her praying that night had helped her remain calm. They both felt God was still honoring her prayers and they would play a significant part in Mitch's life for the long run.

Vonda's eyes fell again onto Ivy and Dan's home where once Victor had lay buried under the driveway. She asked God to comfort and strengthen Victor's family and friends. Since she would always have that visual reminder, just across her back yard, she could see herself praying for all of them for years to come.

Leaning back in her rocker she continued to scan the line of new homes.

A few moments passed and she leaned her head completely back and looked up at the white clouds in the sky.

Almost immediately she caught her breath as a beautiful swarm of butterflies fluttered just above her. There must've been thirty in all colors and shapes. They hovered above her for several moments before gently swooping down around her. They enveloped her as she laughed aloud before they collectively arose and swept away like an amazingly beautiful wind.

Vonda had never had such a thing happen before.

She couldn't help but think it might've been Stanley and his heavenly friends paying her a visit.

V.S. Gardner dreamed of being a published author from childhood and all through the years of caring for her family and working.

Her creative outlets include; writing poetry, personal letters and journaling. In 2020 when her life became less hectic she was excited to achieve her lifelong dream with the publication of her first book A KILLING ON HARDEE STREET.

The book setting echoes her home in beautiful South Carolina. The story centers on a mysterious disappearance amid new relationships, comforting memories and strong faith.

When not writing she enjoys reading, coloring, photography and music.
Her favorite pastime is spending time with family and friends.
She holds to the belief that life's greatest treasures are found in relationships.
She enjoys relaxing at the ocean or the mountains, exploring local points of interest and trail walking with her best friend/husband.
She is grateful for being so very blessed.

Readers are invited to contact V.S. Gardner at vsgbooks2020@gmail.com.